GOOD STORIES REVEAL as much, or more, about a locale as any map or guidebook. Whereabouts Press is dedicated to publishing books that will enlighten a traveler to the soul of a place. By bringing a country's stories to the English-speaking reader, we hope to convey its culture through literature. Books from Whereabouts Press are essential companions for the curious traveler, and for the person who appreciates how fine writing enhances one's experiences in the world.

> "Coming newly into Spanish, I lacked two essentials—a childhood in the language, which I could never acquire, and a sense of its literature, which I could."

> —Alastair Reid, *Whereabouts: Notes on Being a Foreigner*

FRENCH FEAST

A TRAVELER'S LITERARY COMPANION

EDITED BY

WILLIAM RODARMOR

WHEREABOUTS PRESS
BERKELEY, CALIFORNIA

Published by
Whereabouts Press
Berkeley, California
www.whereaboutspress.com

Distributed to the trade by PGW / Perseus Distribution

Library of Congress Cataloging-in-Publication Data

French feast : a traveler's literary companion /
edited By William Rodarmor.
    p.   cm. — (Traveler's literary companions ; 22)
        ISBN 978-0-9827852-1-8 (alk. paper)
        ISBN 978-0-9827852-2-5 (digital)
  1. Short stories, French—Translations into English.
2. French fiction—21st century—Translations into English.
            3. France—Fiction.
        I. Rodarmor, William.
            PQ1278.F73   2011
      843'.0108--dc22   2011013756

5 4 3 2 1

Contents

MAIN COURSES: FAMILY

LIBATIONS: FANTASY

DESSERTS: LOVE AND SEX

Introduction

The book you are holding is a smorgasbord of flavors and situations, from the mouth-watering smell of frying onions to the sweet temptation of caramelized sugar and almonds, set in often surprising circumstances. But none of the thirty-one stories in *French Feast* is really about food; they're about people. The writers in this collection are framing, through food and our connections with it, some of the most fundamental questions of human existence: who are we, where have we come from, where are we going?

Food can both connect people and estrange them. The tradition of breaking bread is a ritual that cements friendship and builds solidarity. But sharing meals can just as easily put people in unequal, even hostile relationships.

Nadine Ribault's story "Tears of Laughter" illustrates

Many of the stories in this collection were suggested by Jean Anderson, an accomplished translator who teaches French at the University of Victoria in New Zealand. Because no good deed should go unpunished, my way of thanking Jean was to make her help write this introduction.—W.R.

this perfectly. A large extended family gathers in a country house for a festive meal, but the tensions between them lie just beneath the surface. A man snacks on chocolate after lunch, covertly criticizing his sister for serving too-small portions. Her quirky decision to replace a traditional cake with her favorite tart is seen as the inconsiderate act of a spoiled daughter. The smallest acts cast prickly shadows.

There is a long tradition of writing about food and its associations in French literature. Rabelais's two sixteenth-century omnivorous giants Gargantua and Pantagruel are among its most memorable characters. Fast-forward three hundred years and the French are still sitting at the table.

Characters eat a great deal in French nineteenth-century novels, and it's easy to understand why. As Priscilla Parkhurst Ferguson writes in her book *Accounting for Taste*: "To the novelist intent on analyzing the relationship between group dynamics and individual psychology, commensality offers a wonderfully exploitable situation. Meals put groups on display, set the scene for dramatic interactions, and foster unexpected relationships across class, gender, and genera-tions." Balzac, a glutton in both eating and writing, focused on a recent innovation, the restaurant. Writes Ferguson: "He fixed on dining as shorthand to chart his characters' relations as they sometimes diligently, often desperately, try to make their way in the world."

But it was Marcel Proust who most memorably put his finger on the emotional subtext associated with, in his case, a little cake and a cup of herbal tea. When young Marcel took that bite of madeleine, he single-handedly launched the recovered memory industry. Whether or not you have actually read *À la recherche du temps perdu*, you know about

Proust's use of taste to reconnect with the past as an iconic experience. "Reinvoked everywhere by cultural commentary from literary criticism to cookie advertisements," writes Ferguson, "the madeleine is surely the most celebrated literary cookie ever baked."

(In her book, Ferguson reprints a 1989 *New Yorker* cartoon that shows Proust getting disappointing news. The writer is lying in bed as a vendor with a coffee cart says, "I'm out of madeleines, Jack. How about a prune Danish?")

In *French Feast*, people are still making their way in the world, but these are now our people and our world. In collecting contemporary stories for the book, we searched the last fifty years or so for literary glimpses of people as they wake, work, love, fight, and, only incidentally, eat. Loosely grouped under menu headings—appetizers, main courses, and so on—these tales show how widely we cast the net.

In the stories "Bresse," "The Taste of New Wine," and "Acacia Flowers," three authors revisit the past in very different ways. The narrator of "Bresse" kills frogs and chickens as a girl and grows up to become a writer. The compassionate doctor in "New Wine" stands midway between kitchen and living room, but also between his patient's life and death. In "Acacia" a man joins his mother in a golden haze of memory, but when he describes feeling a sudden stab of longing, we realize she is dead.

Some of the book's stories are ostensibly about food, but actually about violence. In "Brasserie," a cozy restaurant is the scene of abuse witnessed and remembered. "Come and Get It" invites an errant lover to a delicious dinner and wild sex—followed by just desserts. In other stories, the cutting edge is subtler, more psychological. "Even Me" and "Cafeteria Wine" are basted with bitterness. "Spinach Should Be Cooked with Cream" and "Here They Are How Nice" lacerate ostensibly happy marriages.

A few of the stories are simply off the wall. In "Beef Steak," the women of an entire town sleep with a teenage butcher in hopes of getting a special cut of meat. If you've ever considered eating your furniture, you'll get some tips from "The Armoire." And you may look at cheese differently after reading "Roll On, Camembert."

Finally, a group of the stories focuses not on what the characters eat, but how. "The Plate Raider" and "Belle du Seigneur" are about manners, good, bad, and excruciating. That's fitting, since they come from a country that values doing the right thing but also looking good as you do it, that prizes both *savoir-vivre* and *savoir-faire*. As Professor Higgins says in *My Fair Lady*, "The French don't care what they do, actually, as long as they pronounce it properly."

Jean Anderson, Wellington, New Zealand
William Rodarmor, Berkeley, California

Preface:
An Amuse-Bouche
from the Editor

If you're French, you love your cabbage. I don't mean the cruciform vegetable that lends an acrid reek to the grittier parts of town. I mean that classic French term of endearment, *Mon petit chou,* "My little cabbage." For those of us not lucky enough to be French, this is more than a linguistic oddity. It's a key to national character.

With the possible exception of the Chinese, there are few other peoples on Earth for whom food is more important. The French spend more than two hours a day eating and drinking, nearly twice as much time as Americans. A U.S. household spends 8 percent of its budget on food; a French one, 14 percent.

Food makes history in France, in legend and in fact. Marie-Antoinette never actually said, "Let them eat brioche." Jean-Jacques Rousseau made that up. But when Charles de Gaulle radioed the French underground that the D-Day invasion was imminent, his message included the key phrase *Les carottes sont cuites.* Literally, this means "the carrots are cooked," and metaphorically, "it's all over." What other nation marches to war in the glow of beta carotene?

If you aren't convinced of the intimate link between food

and the French language, try to describe cooking without it. France practically invented our lexicon: entrée, quiche, escargot, crêpe, hors d'oeuvre, petit fours, Béarnaise, baguette, croque-monsieur, vinaigrette, paté, maitre d', sous chef, even the word *cuisine* itself! Not to mention French fries, French toast, and French onion soup.

Far from the kitchen, French food words pop up in the most unexpected places. Here are two of my favorites. First: If you're a besotted lover gazing helplessly at the object of your affections, you're said to *regarder avec des yeux de merlan frit,* "looking with the eyes of a fried whiting," a fish otherwise absent from romantic literature. (Anglo-Saxons make "cow eyes" at each other.) Second: When the French mean, "Who do you think you're kidding?" they might say, *Et mon cul, c'est du poulet?* How a Frenchman's ass came to be made of chicken is a topic best left for another day.

Even when language fails, food finds a way. For years my friend Toby Golick and her husband used to spend part of every summer in a village in the south of France. Despite her rudimentary French, Toby and the local butcher found an enjoyable way to communicate when she went shopping. She would point to a cut of meat and the *boucher* would make the sound of the animal it came from. For fans of French onomatopoeia, I offer the following list:

Cow: *meuuuuhhhh*	Turkey: *glou-glou*
Pig: *grouik-grouik*	Duck: *coin-coin*
Sheep: *bêêêêê*	Chicken: *cot-cot*

For this and many other reasons, I dedicate this collection of stories to Toby Golick. Food really speaks to her.

William Rodarmor

Bresse
Chantal Pelletier

THE MOUTH, FOR EATING, and words to talk about eating. At the table, Bressans talked about what they were eating, had eaten, dreamed of eating. In the evenings, as they played tarot while cooking waffles or flour omelets, they entertained themselves by describing creams, sauces, roasts, pâtés, wedding and mocha cakes. They would ruminate their food, running it through their mouths over and over again, savoring it a thousand times.

Was it from an atavistic fear of going hungry? The Bresse region used to be isolated by swamps, and what could be

---

CHANTAL PELLETIER (1949–) is a versatile writer who loves food. Raised in Lyons, she has studied psychology, toured as an actress, and written for film and television. "I've always been hungry and always been restless," she says. Her body of work includes thrillers, such as *Tirez sur le caviste* (2007) and *Le Chant du bouc* (2000, tr. *Goat Song*), novels like *La Visite* (2003) and *Le squatt* (1996), as well as poems and essays. This essay is from her collection *Voyages en gourmandise* (2007), a part of the "Exquis d'écrivains" series she edits for Nil.

---

grown there was the sole means of subsistence. There was nothing to sell, and not a penny to buy anything with. The slightest meteorological cataclysm could spell famine. A killer frost, a crop-crushing hailstorm, or a drought that turned the fields to dust would drive Bressans to eat dogs, cats, maybe even people. They would wander, pale and skeletal, crazed enough to kill for a scrap of sustenance, to drown themselves with their children, or to cross the Saone River and attack the Macon hillsides, gnawing like animals on wild salsify and beans.

All this happened in a time beyond remembering, but the images of those tragedies still haunted Bressans in the 1950s and '60s. The obsession with shortage accompanied those who "went to the city," like my parents. I haven't forgotten it.

The imperious recitation was a prayer, an act of faith. Food and faith were one and the same. Baptisms, marriages, and first communions were excuses for banquets that would go on for two or three days. The local sausages called *rosette* and *jésus* were more venerated than the Virgin Mary and the Son of God. The good Lord himself was bread: "Take and eat, this is my body; drink, this is my blood."

Lists of dishes and foods were constantly being recited. Those lists! Language at the very birth of language, the oral tradition of the poor, part nursery rhyme, part pagan prayer.

The Bressans were proud of their cuisine. "That's something the rich will never have! They can't cook the way we can. Poor rich people! They're so full of fine speeches, they don't have any room for fine food. They're no happier than we are. Better a good full plate than a good long speech."

Exiled to the city in search of work, my parents liked

to say, "We aren't from around here." But I was proud to be born in Lyons, the center of the world since it was the heart of all good things to eat. Frogs, snails, whitebait from the Saone, poultry, of course—the very best, as everyone knew—and many other Bressan delicacies that made Lyons cooking so wonderful, as other treasures enriched the surrounding regions: sumptuous Dauphiné gratin, Burgundy beef, Beaujolais and Rhone Valley wine. I knew how lucky I was!

Eating well, a privilege of the poor and a family birthright, represented wisdom. Great cooking is born of repeated shortages, which spark the colossal work of metamorphosis.

When I was a child, you didn't count the time spent preparing meals—that was what made them good. Preparations for an ordinary Sunday lunch would start days in advance or, at the very latest, the evening before. Each step took as much time as necessary: desalting, blanching, raising, seasoning, reducing.

Cooking was high culture, with its rules and rituals. Unless they were fools, people proved themselves to be creative, economical, and inventive at the stove. A kind of food psychometric recognized women's skill and culinary IQ. Men's too—Bresse fathers and husbands often lent a hand. There was no choice; preparations were lengthy, so they had to be shared.

We spent hours catching frogs, then days pulling the twitching bodies from a full burlap bag, one by one. Every so often a belly with two legs in yellow-and-green pajamas would go hopping down the garden path, and I had to run to catch these beheaded monsters. The frog was gutted, cleaned, and "undressed"—the thick, shiny skin was yanked down from the slit throat to the feet. The frog's legs were then dredged in flour and fried in hot butter with garlic and parsley.

Time wasn't measured, but the food budget was carefully calculated, and it scrupulously followed the rhythm of the seasons. We did canning whenever a given crop was yielding well. Tomatoes, beans, jams, jellies, pickles, and fruit in syrup or brandy all went into jars to be opened later, during the Earth's winter repose. We avoided buying things, we cooked with leftovers, we used everything.

In Lyons, because my parents worked in a meat and preserves plant, we were allowed to share the lengthy annual ritual of making the headcheese called *svi*.

You took a pig's head, deboned and cleaned it, then cooked it for hours in a large stewpot with salt, pepper, spices, and carrots. You patiently minced the meat, then poured it and its broth into bowls lined up in an unheated shed. As they cooled, they gave off a smell that would make you dizzy.

Each bowl gradually became covered with a thick white layer. You carefully scraped it off with a spoon, then unmolded the perfectly shaped, glittering dome. This was cut into slices and served with baked potatoes. We ate mosaic masterpieces composed of pink, brown, and cinnamon-colored pieces of meat, crescents of carrots, and commas of pearly cartilage, all held in a bronze-flecked transparency. The combination of the cool, savory jelly and the hot baked potato was the luxury of our winters. It cost only the infinite time we had devoted to making it.

Before the miracle of mortgage credit put us in debt for twenty years in exchange for a cramped apartment with cardboard walls, we lived in the Montplaisir neighborhood of Lyons, in the toiletless ground-floor unit of a building owned by the company my parents worked for. My father cultivated its garden, a bit of his native Bresse in the heart of the city, spending all the free time he could spare from his weekly sixty hours of work at the plant.

Hoeing, weeding, fertilizing, sowing, planting: I knew the cost of a green bean or a tomato. I never believed that vegetables came from refrigerator bins or grocery store displays. I knew they were born of a long, respectable cycle, and that it was absolutely forbidden to waste them. Wasting food was a mortal sin.

I can't help but continue to obey this moral lesson today. I still suck the flesh from under fish gills, gnaw on cheese crusts, crack chicken heads and feet on the increasingly rare occasions when I encounter them, chew the soft, satiny cartilage of poultry, suck the marrow out of tiny bones—and tremble with horror at our overflowing garbage cans.

Is the abundance of garbage proportional to the lack of subtlety in eating? After a meal at my parents', very little was left over. There was no complicated packaging and practically everything was used. We ate the scraps and the offal, and used the bones for bouillon and the blood for black pudding.

This cycle fascinated me. When my father would bring home a calf's head in preparation for some notable feast, I would watch for hours as it was being prepared while daydreaming about the calf frisking around somewhere without its head, like the headless frogs I had chased. (Those years seem all to have been marked by visions of decapitated animals.) I didn't feel at all sorry for the calf. Its most enviable fate was to wind up on my plate, covered with a nice *gribiche* sauce. We only eat well that which we love, and we only love what we can eat. I cherish the memory of those calves, whose heads fed our feasts: their silky coats, their trembling legs, their large, damp eyes shaded by long lashes. On my grandmother's farm, mine was the hand that gave them the bottle as soon as they were weaned. Their thick pink tongues would lick my fingers, their warm, slippery gullets would swallow my hand up to the wrist, suckling it so greedily it almost hurt. I was sometimes afraid I would disappear into the sucking void, but the pleasure was so strong I couldn't wait to do it again. I discovered the mysteries of biology though that initial, overwhelming, carnal contact. Hot, throbbing organs hid under the smooth fur, the velvety muzzle, the opalescent skin, the pale flesh. Soft, yielding, spongy masses blazed in the night of bodies. I touched them whenever I pulled a handful of bloody, sticky guts from a plucked chicken, dripping with bile or egg yolk. The sight of these glistening viscera didn't disgust me. It was natural.

Our way of cooking was a far cry from those television shows that promote combining ready-to-cook ingredients. The gastronomic alchemy we practiced started at the very beginning of the cycle.

The things I love to eat were born of blood, of guts, of the throat slitting and slaughtering I witnessed—the red spurting from a pig's throat being bled for blood sausage or from the neck of a rabbit hung by its fur on a hook. Dying and eating were the two ends of the same cycle, and I sensed

Gribiche sauce is a cold, mayonnaise-style egg sauce.

that my writing career would someday find the mysteries of nourishing, friendly flesh in victims and cadavers.

Because words, all words, were tied to food. Not only the spoken word, but the written word as well.

For the members of my family, reading was only useful for deciphering menus at banquets, restaurant menus, or the ingredients of a recipe. My parents, peasants exiled to the city as newlyweds, owned just one book: a big recipe book with a red cover. "If we want to get by, we have to cook," my mother used to say, as she showed off her gastronomic Bible. "With the price of steak what it is, we aren't about to buy it every day."

To my parents, whose language was a mix of Bresse patois and approximate French spoken with a drumroll accent, books were like thin, not very nourishing soup. But so what? They weren't going to fill your stomach, said my father. His motto was, "Better to do more than you say than to say more than you do," which pretty well summed up the way these taciturn peasants thought. Words weren't messengers, but traitors. "Talking like a book" was a sin of vanity, the sign of a show-off.

I brought books into our home as prizes I had won at school. That's when I started to glimpse a world beyond our apartment window. Beyond the stewpots, was there salvation, an elsewhere, other dreams to be devoured?

My most important memory is of buying a dictionary. So many words, treasures, suddenly, the world at my feet, a feast of words, whose matchless flavor was worth any banquet.

In elementary school, my first essay assignment was to write a description. I decided to list ingredients of a vegetable soup. The ruler of morning, noon, and evening meals, soup was my first landscape, my first escape, my first character, with its colors, consistencies, bouillon eyes, vermicelli hairs, and tapioca pearls.

At my grandmother's in the country, "Soup's on!" meant it was time to eat *la sope*. Vegetable soup, green watercress or orange pumpkin; fatty pot-au-feu; cool, minimalist broth on summer evenings: pieces of dried bread sprinkled with creamy milk at cellar temperature that formed a thick skin when it was left to sit. The milk and bread was called *fraisée* because it refreshed and revived you on summer evenings full of wasps and the smell of cut hay.

Each season had its soup. Tomato soup made from the coulis we'd canned, thickened with flour. The soup into which you tossed roadside weeds, thistles, and carrot tops. Then there was the delicious *royale*, with its big chunk of larding bacon—not those pathetic strips of supermarket bacon, but real fleshy bacon with delicate streaks of white, pink, and purple.

I have given up larding bacon, but retain an insatiable taste for soup. Divine soup like the *sopa di pollo* I enjoyed in Chavin, in the Peruvian Andes, after days spent crossing the Cordillera Blanca in a truck; the *soupe au pistou* that Claude cooks when beans are in season; my friend Taka's miso soup; Mireille's bouillabaisse; Serge's gazpacho; Iolande's ginger-orange soup; M. Tranh's shrimp and lemongrass soup . . . Lists, always more lists, that wearisome obsession with naming good things because you might forget them.

The main soup eaten at my grandmother's was impossible to forget. It was made with grilled corn-flour *gaudes*. This was down-home food, invented by our ancestors and ours alone. People say Bressans were called "yellow bellies" not because of the malaria from Bresse's soggy Dombes, or the kernels of corn found in our chickens' omnivorous gizzards (the best in the world), but because of the color of our soup. We were corn eaters.

To make the soup, you used *truqui*—pronounced by rolling your r: trrrrrruqui!—a patois word meaning corn (it's *blé d'Inde* in Quebecois French), brought from the New World by the Spanish during the reign of Louis XIV. It came from abroad, though for the Bressans this didn't mean America, but Turkey.

I would later discover that in Central American culture man was born of corn, that primordial seed. Even today, when I crunch corn flakes or tortillas, or polenta or tamales melt on my tongue, I am transported back to the shafts of sunlight cast by gaudes onto the foggy plains of Bresse. I, too, believe in the corn god.

The name came from *gaude*, a reseda used to make yellow dye, and we loved the warm ocher color. The plural—gaudes—showed how important they were to people of Bresse, who had so often gone hungry. Whether they ate them as soup, dessert, or main course, as long as there were gaudes, Bressans were less fearful of doing without.

To make the flour that was at the base of their preparation, you took kernels of *maïs au lait*—milk corn—toasted them in the oven, then ground the golden seeds in the fin-

Gaudes is a cornmeal porridge that was once the traditional evening meal in Burgundy, Franche-Comté, and Bresse.

est millstone of the impressive mill that straddled the river below the courtyard. On that day, the three-story building would give off a delicate smell of grilled nuts, warm stone, and dry leaves.

Stored in a canvas bag, this platinum-colored powder was slowly sprinkled into a pot full of water from the spring that spurted from a pipe stuck in the rock in the middle of the farm, until the mixture had the consistency and color of the setting sun. Over a low flame, the paste would slowly thicken, then sigh and yawn. As soon as we were old enough, we begged to be allowed to stir this boiling lava, an excuse to watch it.

At the last minute you added a big spoonful of strong-tasting farm butter, redolent of the stable and fresh grass, and stamped with the flowers from the wooden mold that had formed it. This block of soft gold sweated in its translucent paper as if it were still working, still alive.

The plate of steaming gaudes in front of me had all the round, warm beauty of the sun. My cheeks bathed in this savory steam, I watched every detail of the changing spectacle as the soup imperceptibly thickened, and a thin, somewhat darker skin formed. Over this delicate skin you poured the thick, foaming, aromatic milk from the evening's milking, and the chilled skin would harden into a tougher, crunchy crust.

You then plunged your spoon into a golden, snow-swept steppe. The mixture in your mouth was icy, burning, liquid, solid, soft, and crunchy, and every spoonful created a new landscape as you dug white lakes and sandy canyons. It was the most beautiful of journeys.

And yet for my very first essay in elementary school—

"Describe a soup"—I didn't dare choose gaudes. I settled for a vegetable soup. Carrots, onions, leeks, potatoes, everything went in. But not through a food mill; it was all chopped fine, minestrone style. What mattered was making the list. Word soup, vegetable soup—this was something I knew.

So writing meant first describing soup, and drawing out its patois ingredients—a pinch of this, a handful of that—to describe feelings and sentiments. For a long time, I thought that only books talked about such things, and I was happy to have books take the central place that food had once occupied.

I loved school, because there I plunged into writing. It became my favorite dish, and when I was far from this stew, I felt bored. So the pen replaced my fork, the keyboard replaced my plate. I sat down at the table and set off on a journey.

Translated by William Rodarmor

The Cuttlefish

Maryline Desbiolles

I ARRANGE THE INGREDIENTS with the pleasure of a child on the first day of school, taking her brand-new supplies out of her pencil case. The bacon (a little more than five ounces), the three onions (I hesitate between the yellow and white, but not for long, for the white ones are fresher, and shouldn't the white accompany my cuttlefish creation like the train of a dress?), garlic (I wrote down one clove, but I put in two, sometimes it pays to be generous in cooking, when it's not compulsive), parsley (sometimes I neglect to add it, sometimes I even forget. Aside from its color, and to be honest, that's already a lot, I have often thought that parsley doesn't have much of an effect on what I sprinkle

MARYLINE DESBIOLLES (1959–) is a French writer who won the Prix Femina in 1999 for her novel *Anchise*. This chapter from *La Seiche* (1998, tr. *The Cuttlefish*) was translated in 2001 by Mara Bertelsen. Each chapter in the book corresponds to a stage in the author's preparation of stuffed cuttlefish, which is like calamari. In the text, "Cinderella's Godmother" refers to a neighbor who fascinated the narrator when she was a girl.

it into, I have found its aroma a little weak compared to mint or divine coriander; but neither mint nor coriander can favorably replace it, they cannot replace it at all; parsley does not assert itself, it doesn't supersede, it doesn't even enhance, but it acts as a go-between, which, in cooking, is worth its weight in gold. Go-betweens build subtle bridges between ingredients that are not in the habit of meeting, in this case perhaps between the bacon, which we are more likely to view as hearty country food, and the salty tentacles from the sea.)

We rarely remember what we have eaten, though we may recall the pleasure we have gotten, or didn't, from the hosts, or even a snippet of conversation. But to taste cooking, and moreover, to actually do it, is a guaranteed way of putting memories in your mouth, mulling them over again, distilling what they are made of and not just having them rest on the tip of your tongue, but salivating them, putting them to the test of the tongue. Turned over and over in the juices of the mouth, the memories are there at the heart of the matter. The tongue of memory, the tongue that has become the center of the body, as it might in a drawing by a small child, the thin, pointy tongues of witches, the plump tongues of friendly fairy tale gnomes, the forked tongues that whet the appetite as much as frighten.

I remember the gesture of a man who, as he nuzzled my hair, suddenly took it voraciously into his mouth. It was a gesture that was almost charming and yet a rare obscenity. It made my skin crawl with a combination of disgust and consent. He drowned himself in my hair as though it hung in long curls down to my hips, he lost himself in it as though it were at once a dark forest with radiant glades, he sank beneath it as though his greatest desire was to disappear forever. He was drowning himself.

And so, I always imagine that women in love have hair that is long and wavy, especially in a dream, in a daydream where you become a lover held captive by her short hair, I always imagine that women in love have hair that is long and wavy, like the tumultuous water that can make you lose your footing at a moment's notice, as much for the woman who bears the river and lets herself be swept away by its irresistible current as for the man who is covered and uncovered to the point of vertigo by the imaginary hair. Only Pelléas saw the hair of Mélisande as boundless, filled with the song of the endless and deadly sea, whereas for Golaud, her hair was only beautiful.

He drowned himself and he drank too. It was a drowning that profoundly quenched his thirst and spurred it on like never before.

I cut the bacon, onions, garlic, and parsley into coarse pieces, then put it all together with the little pile of heads and tentacles; with my chopper I mince it as much as I can, as finely as possible. I could use the electric mincer, but I don't like the mush that comes out. Besides, I like the movement I impose on the chopper, a little awkwardly, for I use it this way only on rare occasions. My chopper, as vigorous as a sickle, joins in the fun; it is quite old, its little wooden handle is all worn, but its blade is flawless because I take care to have it sharpened regularly.

Cinderella's Godmother, who wanted to get rid of it, gave it to me long before she had made me taste her stuffed cuttlefish. She herself did not turn up her nose at mincing machines, food processors, or vegetable presses. And she always loved and admired cars, which had been a big event in her childhood. Her modern tastes ended there, however, for in everything else, her conservatism bordered on the reactionary.

When I was a child and we were neighbors, I nevertheless saw her as the epitome of originality. She could have been my young grandmother, but she did things that other women her age did not normally do—not my real grandmother at any rate. She knew how to fish, recognized birds by their song, killed pigeons by holding their heads under their wings—suffocating them in their own heat—something which never ceased to horrify and amaze me. She was tiny and slim but didn't hesitate when it came to unloading construction materials her husband brought home in his big truck, and which they sold from the storage area under the house where swallows sometimes nested. She was very pretty and her little body was very well shaped. Everything about her seemed lively and firm, even her black, curly, or rather crimped hair—almost glistening, looking almost waxed—that she held back from the sides of her face with two invisible pins and some green scented cream.

Most important, she cooked regional food; we were from elsewhere and my parents, who had just arrived recently, continued to eat as they had before. At her house, whatever was simmering filled the nose with rosemary and black olives, the sharpness of which was softened in the cooking process, at my neighbor's you ate raw vegetables swimming only in olive oil, which, exotic as it was, for me immediately became a must in all recipes. I fell in love with its marvelous color first of all, its sweet, strong smell; I even love it when it is rancid, a few drops to flavor the evening's soup. I didn't ask my mother to change her cooking habits, but I never missed a chance to sit myself down at my neighbors' table, which I could just barely see over, greedily observing each one of their gestures, only rarely tasting one of their dishes, but latching onto all the words they used to name and describe them.

But as soon as her gaze left her plate, or to be exact, the perimeter of her garden and the garden that was for her much bigger than the surrounding countryside, the neighbor became dishearteningly conventional. You could say that her views became narrower as her field of vision grew larger. As I grew up and began to take a look at the world outside the garden walls, I learned how much her conversation revolved around the commonplace, conversation that, until then, I had always found invigorating because I was captivated not only by her rich vocabulary (she took pains to speak excellent French) but also by the images and certain colorful pronunciations she used that were strange to me. I was delighted when she said *dace* for *days*, or the opposite, *zlip* for *slip*. She was a little precious when she said these words, sure that her pronunciation was right while everyone else's was wrong. And that's when something almost imperceptible took shape, and it took me my whole childhood to realize that she was a bit narrow-minded.

I need to mince, mince as much as I can everything that ends up separating us, to find the little juice that spurts out, the juice that bathes unborn words, pre-word juice, juice we spit into the wind, as insolent as the first day we were confined, my neighbor and I, immured in our own wonders.

Translated by Mara Bertelsen

Fruits & Vegetables

Anthony Palou

MY FATHER USED TO GET UP every day at three in the morning. After buying his produce from the wholesalers, he would come back home around six to fry himself some eggs and herb sausages, which he dipped in stale mustard in an empty Pyrex jar that would later become my tooth-brush glass. The trouble with sausages at that hour is their greasy smell, which slowly, stubbornly crawled upstairs. The sticky essence of *chipolata* or *merguez* would climb the steps, anointing the banister, walls, and ceilings. It made my mother in her bedroom nauseous. While he ate, Papa watched the transistor radio the way you watch a televi-sion. He stared at the radio waves, his already tired eyes

---

ANTHONY PALOU (1956–) is a French writer and a jour-nalist at *Le Figaro* newspaper. He won the 2000 Prix Décembre for his debut novel, *Camille*. This excerpt is adapted from his semiautobiographical 2010 novel *Fruits & legumes,* which won the Prix des Deux Magots in 2011. It takes a nostalgic look back at his family's life in Brittany in the 1970s, as bustling local mar-kets faced the advent of frozen food and chain supermarkets.

fixed on the Philips. Then, after a brief but careful reading of the sports and racing pages of *Ouest France* while on the toilet—its flush was his departure anthem—he drove to the market hall without a word, because he had no one to talk to. Maman went back to sleep. I listened, my nose still full of toxic fumes, as the garbage collectors emptied our cans. For my entire life, there was a time zone difference between Papa and me. My father was a fruit and vegetables man.

To start our 2CV Citroën van in the gloomy morning air, you used an odd button to the right of the steering wheel. You had to pull it out between your index and second finger while energetically pumping the clutch pedal. Later on, we had the same problem with an Ami 6. The van coughed like a consumptive and woke the whole neighborhood. Sofinco, our ill-tempered dachshund—twelve years old and named after a credit union—would howl like a stuck pig, while our neighbor Nicole Le Bihan threw open her shutters and screamed. A slatternly, big-bosomed redhead on the wrong side of forty, she was the mother of a half dozen male and female degenerates she'd had with a former dyer who threw himself under the Quimper-Pont l'Abbé bus one morning. It was understandable; sadness had overtaken his meager conjugal joys. Nicole had no rival in the art of the insult, and Sofinco, who was all excited, continued howling shrilly. Meanwhile, my father, his cap pulled down on his head and a Gitane between his lips, made his getaway.

In my dreams, I envied Papa. I envied him moving through dawn's yellowish haze as I burrowed deeper into my pillow to protect myself from the cold, razor-sharp northern gusts he must be facing. As soon as he came back, around eight or eight thirty in the evening, I would often take his place at the wheel of the gray 2CV, imitating his driving, moving the gearshift with its big black knob in the center of the bare-bones dashboard (a speedometer and two gauges). I wanted to breathe that curious smell of diesel, dark tobacco, and fresh fruit, and in some seasons, the reek of slightly rotten cauliflower that seeped from the van's metal side panels. With its sagging seat, worn-out springs, strapped-down canvas top, and skinny steering wheel, I covered kilometer after imaginary kilometer, basking in the pleasure of feeling grown-up.

The 2CV's brakes weren't very reliable. Nothing in that rattletrap was. When you parked the heroic Citroën on a street as steep as ours, you had to turn the wheels to the curb in order to wedge them. And what was bound to happen eventually happened one evening when I thoughtlessly released the hand brake and ran over Sofinco, who was lying in the gutter a few yards downhill, calmly licking his balls. I felt the van go over a bump. In a panic, I finally managed to stretch my leg far enough to reach the brake pedal and stop. I could see him stiffly lying there, dying. He whined, looking at me with sad eyes still full of kindness. I took his muzzle in one hand and clapped the other over his nose until he suffocated. Unable to breathe, he gave a limp twist and died. I had joined the world of killers. On June 14, 1972, at the age of seven.

Was I going to hide my crime? I didn't really get the chance. My mother accused my father of not setting the hand brake. Papa objected, but without much conviction. I went upstairs to my room feeling vaguely disgusted. I was allowing my father to be falsely accused. Then I had, not a revelation, but a question: why wasn't he fighting back?

Wasn't he the hero I heard bravely waking up every morning before anyone else? We never spoke of this family episode again. Papa started wedging wooden blocks under the Citroën's front wheels for safety, and the canine species was absent from our house for a long time.

The van that Papa set out in was a modern mule that pitched like a square-rigger in a full gale. At times the rear bumper scraped the pavement under the weight of the produce crates.

At the start of summer, my father set up a potato peeler in the garage that looked like a cement mixer. You dumped in dozens of kilos of Sirtemas potatoes from Moirmoutier or Amincas from Ré and sprayed them with a hose while the serrated bin spun around, making a hell of a racket. You then poured the peeled spuds into big plastic buckets of water. When four, five, or six of these were full, they were all loaded into the van, which sagged under the weight of the starchy mass. I would face my own dose of potato chores a few years later when I started to work in the market hall during school vacations. The number of sacks of potatoes I've carried! Tons of BF 15s, Bintjes, Rattes, Monalisas, Spuntas, Sambas, Estimas, Manons, Pompadours, and Rosines. Enough potatoes to never want to eat them again, fried or mashed.

What a neighborhood pain in the ass Papa must have been, between his 2CV and his potato peeler, whose soggy water drained into the gutter of the rue des Dardanelles where we lived, in Quimper, Finistère prefecture, 29000.

Papa did his buying before the market hall opened. The wholesalers unloaded the merchandise from their trucks in an atmosphere that felt like a black market. There were just five wholesalers: Bégot & fils, Nature et Vie, Terre de France, Les Fruitiers Bretons, and, a little later, Bioprogrès. The retailers bought fruit and vegetables from them that weren't usually grown in Brittany. For their part, the local truck farmers sold lettuce, shallots, onions, radishes, leeks, strawberries from Plougastel, and raspberries from the garden. My father preferred to deal with the truck farmers. It was easier to bargain with them, to get three crates of zucchini for the price of two, the way at Bab el-Oued you can buy three Persian carpets made in North Africa. A nice shot of dry muscadet down the hatch greased the negotiations. The orders varied according to the day of the week.

There were three big market days: Wednesday, Friday, and then Saturday, which was D-Day and Operation Overlord, when the old ladies, the heads of households, loaded their baskets or shopping carts for the big Sunday lunch. From Friday on, the orders started coming in as people calculated, evaluated, got excited. The worst was the day before a holiday: Easter Sunday and Easter Monday, Christmas and turkey with chestnut stuffing, then New Year's with the leg of lamb and beans of all sorts: fayots, dried beans, haricots, and mojettes from Vendée.

I can still hear the ladies impatiently grumbling: "Monsieur Coll, you won't forget to save some flageolets for me, will you? Chevirer beans, right, Monsieur Coll?"

"Of course not, Madame Le Nir, I've made a note," Papa would answer, a pencil behind his ear.

"What about me, Monsieur Coll, and my special endives? You know my son and his little family are coming, I haven't seen them for six months, so just imagine, they're coming from so far away, New Caledonia, you know my big boy is a soldier, don't you? Don't forget my pears either, Monsieur Coll."

"Of course, of course, I won't forget your endives, Madame Kerdoux, and say hello to your husband for me."

"Can you deliver that before six o'clock?"

"Of course, Madame Kerdoux, before six o'clock. Consider it done."

And so forth. He saw some sad cases, my father. There was one I remember as if it were yesterday: Roberte de Kermadec, a local character who owned a 17th-century château on the Odet River and a stud farm. An aristocratic lady whose account at the Credit Agricole was shot and whose stock portfolio was in the toilet. She would appear around one forty-five in the afternoon, when the merchants were discreetly adding up their receipts and starting to close the stalls. You could hear la Kermadec then, tapping the rough tiles of the market hall with her cane like a blind woman, in search of carrot tops, radish and turnip greens, crushed parsley or tired chives, rotten oranges and tomatoes. The old lady was famous for her stinginess, and people muttered behind her back. "She says they're for her horses. My eye! They're for her soup tonight!"

The banks of the Odet. The famous "château route," the tourist guides call it, where aristocrats built manor houses in the 16th and 17th centuries: Bodivit, Lanniron, Keraval, Perennou, Kerbennez, Kerambleiz. Once lords of the manor, they're still called "the river people" today.

You should have seen the market hall before the first customers arrived. It already smelled of the sharp sweat of the porters, big, husky guys loaded down with stuff moving in a strange ballet whose only music was the squeak of wheels and bursts of voices. The most animated area was always the fishmongers'. Marcel Le Corre, a fish wholesaler from Guilvinec, wasn't the quiet type. The moment he stepped out of his salt-corroded refrigerated Ford Taunus, he would start screaming through his reddish mustache about Common Market taxes, the price of sole, the price of bluefin tuna, which wasn't endangered yet, the cod quotas, the small size of sardines, and the large size of his assistant's buttocks. "Goddamn fucking mother of God, will you move that big ass of yours?" And Nicole would move, parking her impressive hindquarters far from her boss's bestial humor.

Marcel's two sons had been fishermen, and were lost in the Irish Sea. Their trawler was never found, much less the two boys, certainly eaten by crabs by now, God rest their souls. Old Marcel was a copper-toned colossus. You'd think he waxed his face every morning. Life had weathered this towering hulk, who demolished the competition with his fresh fish and his gift of gab. Big talk attracts customers, and that brings more customers—it's a law. My father liked Marcel a lot, and it was best to be on good terms with him. Marcel's enemies couldn't long endure his flights of lyricism. While not exactly a troubadour, he attained well-orchestrated peaks of vulgarity at the Commerce, Bretagne, Central, Pénalty, Narval, and Menhir bars. Always up for another round, Marcel must have had a hollow leg and a rubber liver. He'd been vaccinated against cirrhosis by years on the open sea, and cholesterol was a concept as foreign to him as drinking water.

Well-meaning people said Marcel had started to drink after the death of his sons. Wrong. He'd started to drink when his wife Louise—Loulou, Louisette—ran off with an Irishman, one Robert O'Connor, who ran a frozen food business. For Marcel, that was real punishment. He, the king of fresh Dover sole, to be cuckolded by a specialist in frozen food! Besides soccer and horse racing, the main topic of conversation between my father and Marcel was the Rungis market, which, they claimed, was sucking in all the best products of the region to benefit the Parisians—*Parigots!* In the summer, as soon as Marcel spotted a car with the telltale license number 75, the blood went to his head. He would lie in wait for them at the market hall. When those morons asked the perennial question, "Was your cod caught today?" he had a salty comeback at the ready: "Why, does it smell like your old lady?" Marcel wasn't the kind of guy you could take just anywhere. I once saw him whack a guy across the face with a ray when the man's five- or six-year-old son put a dirty finger on one of Marcel's Iroise lobsters' antennas. The police had to intervene, and the cops themselves nearly had their kepis knocked off with a backhanded monkfish. Marcel set sail for the last time in February 1992, at the age of 77. A heart attack, a few days after the Maastricht treaty was ratified.

At the Guilvinec church, Nicole wept for her boss with all the tears in her body. They say he was buried in his boots and pea jacket, with his pipe and two bottles of Sancerre in the coffin.

My father was never that crazy about fruits or vegetables, or even business, for that matter. So how did he become a businessman? Let's say he continued my grandfather's work the way the son of a soldier carries on a military tradition that he doesn't believe in. The number of priests is falling because they don't have children. Each profession reproduces the way animals do. My friends who studied medicine or dentistry were all sons of doctors or dentists, and I didn't have to read Pierre Bourdieu to figure that out. So Papa became a fruit and vegetable seller as a matter of heredity. Except that the lifeblood of business didn't circulate in his veins very well. It tended to stagnate and clot.

My father was born on Friday, June 21, 1940, the date of France's surrender. The heavy hands of the Laennec hospital clock pointed to three thirty. In a Compiègne forest clearing not from Rethondes, where the 1918 armistice had been signed on November 11, Hitler got his revenge and France her humiliation. At the Île de Sein, fishermen were setting sail to go join de Gaulle in London.

Those were the lean days of potatoes and root vegetables. Soup during the week, ratatouille on holidays. When you started to see the bottom of the pot, you stretched the soup with water and put pieces of bread or boiled vermicelli into it. Specks of grease floated on the surface; we called them "cow eyes." But Grandpa Antonio hadn't left his native Mallorca to spend evenings hunched over a cracked, empty bowl in France. He didn't like twiddling his thumbs, and he didn't like being poor. He wanted to be a businessman, own a prosperous business, become solidly middle class. He wanted to give the name "Coll" a respectable ring.

Grandpa started with a rickety wheelbarrow and an idea. The idea had a name: René. René was a prematurely retired tomato grower who'd wound up in a wheelchair and couldn't cultivate his fields. A childless widower, he gave

Grandpa the use of the farm. For his part, Grandpa rolled up his sleeves, grabbed a hoe and spade, and planted tomatoes, carrots, leeks, zucchini, eggplants, radishes, endives, and lettuce. In exchange, he had to be nice to René, wheel him around, share a bottle of wine when the old man felt low, cook him stew twice a week, play nursemaid.

The wheelbarrow made a funny, rusty noise as it clattered along the hard roadside dirt. The old commune of Egué-Armel was five or six kilometers from downtown Quimper. Every morning, Grandpa took the same wandering route in the darkness, following the jerky light of an acetylene lamp tied to the front of the wheelbarrow. He set up shop by laying a pair of planks on sawhorses under a shed roof near the market hall. His neighbors on either side were an accordion player who pretended to be blind and a poultry seller who was always filthy. Then it was show time.

Grandpa carefully lined up his crates and arranged the vegetables with the artistry of an impressionist painter. The red of the tomatoes, damp with morning dew, set off the coral pink of the peppers. Pale yellow onions joined the green of cucumbers and eggplant stems in a pastoral vision of an autumnal path. The orange of bunches of carrots stood out boldly next to the purplish mauve of boiled beets and the earthy black of radishes freshly pulled from the ground. An inspired designer, Grandpa was painting still lifes.

The prices he chalked up on the cross-ruled blackboards were pretty approximate: his old hanging scales gave the weights of the produce as best they could.

The first days were the longest. The vegetables slowly wilted under the sun or the rain as Monsieur Coll, Quimper-Corentin fruit and vegetables man, patiently watched.

Meanwhile, his neighbor Maurice the poultry seller was cutting chickens' necks, slicing vertebrae, lifting lungs with fingers black with grime, excising the anal ring, then magically cutting them up—where did those gross fingers find such sudden grace?—without tearing anything or breaking the liver bile sac, before tying them up. Rarely did one of Maurice's customers turn to Grandpa's display to buy a tomato or a bunch of parsley.

A few dull coins languished in the accordion player's beret. Skinny dogs wandered over to piss on the sawhorses, and were booted away. Then it was time to pack and load up the merchandise. His pockets empty, Grandpa trundled his poverty along the road home. Lunch was silent, eaten in a kitchen so narrow it was hard to get around the table. It was bouillon—today, yesterday, tomorrow, and the day after. Hmph. Grandpa poured his soup from one bowl to another to cool it, then sprinkled it with pepper. No salt. He drank two fingers of wine, muttered, "Not bad, for mouthwash," and wiped his lips.

Later, after a nap, he would wear out his knees working the earth, hoeing and harvesting in the eager heat or stubborn wind. Sitting at his window, René would squint though a pair of Harold Lloyd glasses perched on his nose, tufts of hair bursting from his wide nostrils. With a short black cape across his shoulders and a seaman's cap on his head, he'd chew tobacco, nodding, dozing, drooling.

But Antonio Coll's business was about to expand as dramatically as a woman eight months pregnant with triplets, all thanks to *sopa mallorquina*. For this, Grandpa pressed his wife into service. My grandmother was docile and obedient, a woman who knew her way around a stove and wasn't afraid of work. A brave Breton recruit, she jumped right in. Not that she lacked personality—far from it—but it was as if her pale eyes had been designed to hide her thoughts. I must now give you the miraculous recipe behind their fortune, the secret code, with the precision of a cat jumping on a mouse. Here is what's on the shopping list. (Be careful not to forget anything; it's a long inventory):

1 leek, diced
1 onion. sliced
3 cloves of garlic, roughly crushed
1 handful of green beans, cut up, and spinach and
    dandelion greens
½ bell pepper (any color)
3–4 florets of cauliflower or broccoli (your choice)
½ of a white cabbage, minced
10–12 Paris mushrooms, sliced
1 hot chili pepper
1 can stewed tomatoes
2 chicken bouillon cubes
Slices of slightly stale bread

Start by pouring yourself a glass of wine, because you'll need all your strength for the coming exercise. In a large stewpot, heat 2–3 tablespoons of olive oil. Add the leek and onion and blanch over low heat, being careful not to scorch them. Dissolve the chicken bouillon cubes in a pot of water. Add the cabbage and garlic. Slowly reduce the liquid, then add four large tablespoons of stewed tomatoes and the chopped pepper. Add enough liquid to moisten the vegetables without covering them. Add the green beans, chili pepper (if it's Zimbabwe bird pepper, be careful; they're hot as hell), salt, the cauliflower or broccoli, mushrooms, spinach and (optional) dandelion greens. Simmer 45 minutes, while you read a book, knit, knit some more, do a crossword puzzle, or listen to the radio or to Tino Rossi singing "Méditerranée." Add bouillon as needed. Ladle the soup into bowls over the bread, which has been patiently waiting. Have some salt handy. Enjoy.

That was how my grandfather made his reputation in the Quimper market hall. Every Saturday, he sold jelly jars full of *sopa mallorquine,* and jar by jar, it kept poverty at bay. Word of mouth became the thick soup's best advertisement. People started lining up, placing orders. Grandma even had to come in to handle the cash box. Monsieur and Madame Coll were greeted with new deference. "Hey, Antonio! Hello, Madame Coll. You look as well as the Good Lord's day is long!"

Maurice and the accordion player were happy at this sudden notoriety, and profited by the queue in front of Antonio Coll's. The customers would buy a chicken thigh or a bit of liver or gizzard from Maurice, and might toss a coin into the hat of the accordion player, who celebrated the morning's end by getting off his old chair and cutting a series of heroic farts.

By the time Grandpa moved from his pathetic sawhorses to a small rented stall in the market hall, he had rebuilt an old Renault Galion delivery van salvaged from the junkyard. He was a born mechanic—I always remember his fingers as stained with grease—and he managed to build himself a van, the external sign of his still-modest wealth. With his foreign accent, his Southern ways, his fits of anger—which soon became as well known as his soup—his quasi-poetic exaltation, and his romantic courage, Antonio rose to become a figure in Quimper society.

The Saint-François market hall was built in 1846, on the site of a former Franciscan monastery that was abandoned during the Revolution. In 1970, it held some thirty businesses, mainly fruit and vegetable sellers. Designed by one Bigot, its architecture is Gothic and simple, a series of gray arches forming a rectangle one hundred by sixty meters.

On August 27, 1976, the Quimper market hall burned down. It was our *Titanic*.

For a week, Papa was as if frozen, turned into a painful pillar of salt. He may have died that day. I saw sadness moving across his face, in his damp eyes. I could see a strange, sepia-tinged movie playing in his head: his stall, his scales, his jackets, the chalkboards where he wrote the prices every morning. All up in smoke. The good times were over. We'd be drinking cold water from now on.

My father stared at the ashes. The butcher stared at the ashes. The pork butcher stared at the ashes. The fishmonger put his hand on the baker's shoulder. They all stood there, looking at the glowing embers, feeling heartsick. Nobody shed any tears; it wasn't done. All that was left were the four scorched, tottering pillars that once held up the handsome building.

Nothing remained of Papa's stall except the charred scales and melted cast-iron weights. The Saint-François market hall had become a glass-littered no man's land. The sausage breakfasts, the shots of white wine at eight in the morning—

all that was finished. Bored stiff, Papa waited for a settlement from the insurance company, which promptly found an error in the contract and announced that compensation for the market hall disaster would be minimal. For long, long months nobody talked much in the Coll household. Lunches and dinners dragged by at the slow rhythm of a pendulum. While the Quimper City Hall looked at more or less imaginary projects and architects' more or less futuristic plans to rebuild the market, I could see Papa succumbing to depression. Toward the end of winter, he sank into a kind of melancholy. Nothing much, just an imperceptible change in the daily rhythm. It was all over.

One Sunday, when my grandparents had come to lunch—gone were the days when we feasted on Belon oysters and roast beef; now we ate sad liver paté and watery pork roast—Grandpa, with his nose in his plate, said he remembered when a lanky old Breton farmer once had a meal with him. His name was Édouard Leclerc, and he was a kind of crazy prophet. His big idea? Mass distribution. Buying and selling in bulk, the way the army did. Stores could give incredible discounts, he said, not to mention a one or two percent year-end rebate on the previous twelve months' purchases. The spread of supermarkets—we called them *centrales* in those days—would be the rot that attacked the foundations of small businesses. A death knell for our way of life.

Translated by William Rodarmor

Pfefferling

François Vallejo

WHEN I WAS ABOUT FIFTEEN, I used to spend my vacations in Switzerland. Not in palaces, exactly, but in pretty good hotels. I was a semi-poor kid, and it may seem like a paradox that a poor person's son should spend as much as three weeks during the summer in a hotel for almost-rich people. I had just read Thomas Mann's *The Magic Mountain*, and it might seem another paradox that a poor fifteen-year-old boy should read something like that. But the poor read what they can, and what they come across. So I felt deeply moved to find myself in Davos-Dorf, in the Grisons, very close to the sanatorium where in the novel Hans Castorp goes to visit his cousin and falls ill himself.

When I wasn't feeling deeply moved, I went hiking in the surrounding mountains, and when I wasn't hiking, I

FRANÇOIS VALLEJO (1960–) is a French novelist whose books include *Les soeurs Brelan* (2010), *Groom* (2003), and *Vacarme dans la salle de bal* (1998). This piece appears in *A Table,* an anthology of food-related stories published in 2004 by Editions Delphine Montalant.

ate—and ate quite a lot. The hotel restaurant was run by a chef of whom the customers all spoke highly, and in every language. The first person to praise this chef in my presence was my neighbor in the next room down the hall, an old woman. She spoke of him somewhat enigmatically: to hear her, the man was never better than when he was cooking for a single client, namely herself, and not for the restaurant's entire clientele.

I wasn't quite sure I understood what the lady was saying, because she spoke very rapid but jerky French with a German accent, and in a quavering voice. She was a very old woman and had taken a liking to me. She wasn't a vacationer here, at least not a vacationer like the Swiss, Austrians, Germans, French, and Britons she pursued with a nonstop flow of conversation in an attempt to escape her isolation. She had lived full-time in the hotel for the previous five years, completely alone, according to a discreet word from the manager. She'd not had a single reported visit, nothing. And yet she was wealthy and a countess, a German countess. My family dubbed her Madame Von, because we couldn't remember her very complicated name.

At mealtimes, Madame Von would arrange to leave her room just as I was crossing my own threshold, would stick with me until we reached the dining room, and sit down at a table next to ours. She continued the dialogue between each bite and judged each dish with an odd mix of admiration and condescension. This veal *émincé* was rich and subtly flavored, she said, but it was nothing compared to what the cook was capable of doing for her. Madame Von annoyed us a little. Either the chef had talent or he didn't; what was the point of denigrating him while pretending to admire his cooking?

"To be at hiz best," the lady claimed, "he needs me."

She and I once spoke about *The Magic Mountain*, and the countess said something that struck me: with what could be gathered on our magic mountain, the chef would outdo himself. I could hardly understand this semi-crazy woman, who was raving to a semi-poor boy. With the rude boldness of a fifteen-year-old, I told her that I didn't see any connection between the cook and the novel I loved.

"Do you vant to take a valk vith me? You vill understand vat I mean."

The idea of walking with me delighted her, since she was sure that a boy of my age would have enough wind not to be left behind by an octogenarian, unlike the wheezing tourists who depended on the ski lifts. And that turned out to be true. I didn't yield an inch to the galloping countess, but only by dint of tremendous effort.

"I vant to show you ze places mentioned in ze book."

By midafternoon, we reached the sanatorium. It was a large, imposing building, all the more impressive when I considered that it had welcomed Thomas Mann himself. But I didn't want to go inside. I was afraid that, like Hans Castorp, I would never come out again. So Madame Von suggested another visit: to the cemetery, which was in the middle of the forest. According to her, the sanatorium's inhabitants—those of today, those of the past, and even those of the novel—were buried there. A place not to be missed, she said. The cemetery was some distance away from everything and surrounded by a low, mossy wall. It was a kind of meadow, and the tombs themselves were overgrown mounds of earth. A vegetable cemetery, not a stony one like ours.

Madame Von strolled across the graves, which were hard to distinguish from the pathways. I felt indignant at her casualness, though I kept it to myself. She would be talking away with her hand on a cross and her foot on a skull or perhaps on a tibia. The countess noticed her young hiking companion's expression and said I was wrong to judge her harshly, because at her age she could afford to be familiar with people who were almost all younger than her, and whose numbers she would join in the very near future.

We walked around for quite a while, as if we were in a public park. Madame Von seemed to be looking for something, an acquaintance perhaps. Then she ran to the north wall.

"Zere zey are! I vas sure I vould find some!" she cried.

She had spotted some mushrooms.

"Come quickly. Vat do you call zem in French? Where I'm from, ve say Pfefferling, like pepper, Pfeffer, see? And you, what do you say?"

"Chanterelles."

"Iss that vat zey are, shantrells? Quick, a big handkerchief."

From her sleeve, she drew a large white handkerchief with red checks.

"Help me. I love zem, shantrells."

We picked chanterelles right off the tombs of the late tuberculosis patients, which seemed very productive: we gathered more mushrooms than I ever had in any French forest. Countess Von knotted up her handkerchief and handed the bulging bundle to the poor frightened boy, who was condemned to carry these mushrooms with their spiky Germanic name.

We went back as if we were just starting out, at a run.

My companion was eager to get back to the hotel. Five thirty was still a good time for a light meal. She went to the kitchen and pounded on the door, shouting like a girl. Taking the handkerchief, she poured its contents onto a work table. The chef was called. She demanded a chanterelle omelet immediately, brought to her room with two plates.

"You vill see, I told you he vas at his best ven he vorks for me only. You vill understand."

No one questioned her orders. This was a regular occurrence, and fixing a meal for Madame the countess in the middle of the afternoon did not surprise or shock the hotel employees. I, on the other hand felt doomed, unable to think of a pretext to escape these chanterelles of death, these fleshy mushrooms swollen with wet and earth and mixed with the rotting flesh of old Davos and *Magic Mountain* TB lungers, a dish being presented to my taste buds as the finest of feasts, and not to be missed.

The omelet was a runny masterpiece. "A real treat," said Madame Von. "Isn't it a treat?" She rambled on about the delicacy of the mushrooms mixed with the unctuousness of the beaten eggs, the nip of the garlic joined to the peppery flavor of the chanterelles, some minced parsley for color, "nothing simpler, nothing greater, that's where you see that the chef is a . . ."

"Yeah, a real treat," I said very quietly, trying not to gag, as I swallowed one small bite at a time of the most disturbing omelet I've ever had to eat. I even tried to put the chanterelles off to the side, covering them with a slice of bread.

"You forgot a little zere," said Madame Von. "So young you are, and going blind already."

I had to finish it all, even mopping the plate with my

bread at the urging of the countess, whose savoir-vivre allowed her to lick such a dish to its last grain of pepper, to the last Pfefferling.

I ran to my room, where I spent long minutes over the toilet, getting rid of the meal.

I had occasion to go back to Davos a few years later. I remembered Madame Von's mushrooms with amusement, and told myself that I would eat them more willingly this time. The hotel manager didn't give me the same room, and in the morning I didn't run into Madame Von. Nor did she appear around nine o'clock at the next table, which was now occupied by a family of four very upright Austrians.

"What? Didn't I tell you?" asked the surprised manager. "Our countess died last autumn. She ordered a mushroom omelet—you know her habits, I believe—and she was found dead the next morning."

"Were the mushrooms poisonous?"

"That's what we were afraid of, but no, there was no sign of poisoning. I think old age and loneliness are far more poisonous than mushrooms."

It was a hot, humid August. I walked to the little cemetery. I knew, because the manager had told me, that the old lady lay in a new grave, under a tree. There were a lot of trees, and I wandered for a long time before stumbling across the countess's already somewhat overgrown tomb. It read, "1890–1977." My gaze strayed across the grass, which was already high. And there in the upper part of the plot, a little to the right, stood a very small chanterelle mushroom. What was the German name again? It was a peppery name, like Madame Von herself: Pfefferling. Her name should have been Madame Von Pfefferling. What should I do? I gently pulled up the chanterelle, and without waiting to return to the hotel—where the chef would certainly not agree as readily to my demand as he had to the caprice of an old German countess, especially for a single mushroom, and a tiny one at that—with no fear of poisoning, relieved of any conventional scruple, with lightness of spirit and filled with gratitude to Countess Von, I swallowed whole the most delicate and the most peppery "shantrell" I've ever eaten.

Translated by William Rodarmor

The Taste of New Wine

Mariette Condroyer

THE GARDEN GATE. A young woman, Agathe, is standing by that gate, wearing a white embroidered dress and an
Italian straw hat and holding a parasol.

A gentle half smile, in this photo from the early 1900s—
the exact date is written on the back of the photo but its
last digit is illegible. Something else was also written there,
probably the month, or maybe a more intimate thought,
carefully erased.

An image to sum up an entire life, some of it legible,
some of it less so, "mad as the mist and snow."

Agathe will remain in that garden for a lifetime, standing
guard near that same tree. How many times in life's seasons
will the water of the river, the Garonne, rise from its bed

MARIETTE CONDROYER (1934–) is a French author
and screenwriter. Her books include the novels *Tous les par-
fums de l'Arabie* (1999), *Mangeur d'âmes* (1998), *Emma Bovary est
dans votre jardin* (1984); and the short story collections *Fugitifs*
(2003) and *Un Après-midi plutôt gai* (1993), which won the Goncourt short story prize. This story appears in her 1997 collection
N'écris plus jamais sur moi.

---

and spread across the drained marshland *palus*, flood the plain of poplars, cross the *route nationale*, pass the church courtyard, and flow into the main street?

Flood season.

Agathe will lean from her second-story window and wave to the people sitting in the boats.

A street turned waterway. Tufts of grass sticking up.

A postcard of this navigable street: two boats, one with a man and his dog, the other with children and their school-teacher; the children are smiling and waving.

Muddy water everywhere, on the city hall steps, on the market stalls, on the walls of Agathe's home, on the stairs, the water only reached the fourth step, a small flood this year, muddy water on furniture not worth carrying upstairs.

But it's not flood season anymore.

Pretty Agathe near the garden gate is now holding a bicycle.

Then another photo in the same place. Agathe has only moved a few yards, the gate is a little farther away in the picture, the upper part of Agathe's face is dark as night, even her eyes. Clouds float above the dazzling hour. "Summer" is written on the back of the photo, with no indication of the place.

Probably another summer. A sweltering one. At that hour there's no one on the main street, and in the sparsely shaded garden the young woman obediently agrees to pose in front of a distant cousin's lens. He's passing through, a relative from the capital who came to see her on vacation. Agathe has just gotten married.

Another image, a blurry one with dark areas, nothing in this one is sharp, the focus was bad. The cousin is learning—he's not an expert in the art of photography. He tried out his new camera this morning already, this time on a *commandeur* with pale eyes, Agathe's beloved husband, the doctor with the red beard.

It's as hot as a greenhouse in the garden, but cool in the house. Visiting hours. In the white hallway waiting room a single patient sits today, or rather slumps. He has already lost his grasp of hours and is now attuned only to his illness, he slumps further, is practically falling when the doctor stands him up and leads him into his office, a room for all pains and all comforting. Healing, operating, pulling teeth, this doctor can do it all, he is interested in your whole being, not just in parts of you. He travels through your depths, accompanies you, holds your hand until the very end.

A door separates the office from the kitchen, a door padded for privacy that doesn't close tightly and sometimes stands ajar.

For a person who is anxious or in pain, this door between the two rooms is important. This door gives onto a time of life, the kitchen and its smells, a place of life, a place of reassuring sounds, the clatter of dishes, snatches of speech. But today the patient came at the wrong time, an inert hour of the afternoon; no meal is being prepared in the next room, the smell of coffee is already long gone. The patient is left with nothing but his pain, that's all he can listen to, its continuing rumble of catastrophe. This particular patient isn't very patient, he's oppressed with forebodings, and that's why he came at an unusual hour so early in the afternoon, in a hurry to find out, but he didn't learn anything more, his trouble merely delayed a few hours. All he wanted to hear from the doctor were a few murmured words, but from the kitchen, that most reassuring of rooms, no comfort came. So he will return in the late afternoon, when dinner is being prepared.

And that evening after the doctor's "Not so good, old man." Less murmured this time. To the patient, this means, "You're dying." He isn't too surprised, he's been warned, this thing he's been dragging around in his body for the last few months is an old story, and after the confirmation of what he already knows, he'll have time to breathe in all sorts of delicious smells from the next room, the kitchen, get drunk on those smells of life because the doctor sometimes goes into that room, he opens the door between them and steps into the kitchen. Is he also in need of comforting, when he is comforting other people?

This patient enjoys those smells of a meal being prepared; that ongoing life close to him has so much sweetness, it's already part of another dimension, a life that seems unreachable, unreal, much more fantastic than this unknown one, this anticipated death so ready to possess him. The other dimension lies more in what he's going to lose, that's where the fantastic is, the breath that can't be held, this "fiction life," this present smell of wine being warmed.

What will they eat at the doctor's tonight? He tries to guess. The pinfeathers of a fowl are being singed, sugar has been poured onto the stove top.

The doctor has left him for a moment for the laughter next door, and he remains lying in the office whose floor is so clean, its walls so white, there he is, an abandoned body, yet less alone, because the door was left ajar. Noises, quick steps, the doctor's young wife is checking the evening menu. The smell of sauces, of simmering game stews. A murmuring agitation, irritation, voices. And frying onions, especially.

The patient is still dreaming of that other place. At last, some positive, reassuring element this evening, after that notion he can't get out of his head . . .

"A matter of days."

Something delirious washes over him, a curious rush of life, a need to seize the passing moment, a maddened crisis of holding on; he hears Agathe's soft voice, a single word, "overcooked," and that "overcooked" gives him the illusion of appetite. Going over the hellish menus for the coming days in his mind. Such a brief instant. And as soon as the door closes and the doctor comes back, he's himself and his pains again, hears only them, like clocks of the final evening, and his bared belly ready to be summoned, his body made loud by fear.

And this patient, this patient who suddenly feels famished, will be given a reprieve, and will tell anyone who will listen that he hung on desperately, to what he doesn't know, "I was hanging on," he repeats.

After that evening of pain and joy, he felt both so good and so bad, having enjoyed the preparation of meals that brought him to the preparation of other pains. That's what he hoped, at least. A few more weeks, an ironic gift, an alternation of discomfort and desires, to make him believe he had the strength to eat and drink, to roast fowl of every plumage and beasts of every kind, he who had felt so weak.

Seated before a clear broth, he recited menus served with

ceremony. Indigestion caused by imagination. Exhausted, nauseated by too many dreams mixed with too many pains, feeling his absolute worst, yet he kept on coming every day to the man who talked about everything except him. He always came when the onions were browning, carefully studying the varied daily menus of the end of summer and the beginning of fall. And in the last days of September, the doctor, the *commandeur* with the light-colored eyes, constantly shuttles between his office and the kitchen, it is grape-harvesting time, and he weighs a sample of new wine from his vineyard, tastes the must, weighs it again, compares it to other years, discusses it, praises it. A whole ceremony that the patient, as a connoisseur, appreciates, an evening ritual during the grape harvest that he wouldn't miss for the world, and certainly not now, his last autumn.

This last autumn, the doctor has never been so lyrical about the fruitiness of a Sauvignon, but otherwise has nothing else to tell him, and will only speak of his small problems, a cold, a scratch, this is a kind of convention between them, the patient didn't come to ask about the other things, he knows everything there is to know about the constant pains that will never leave him. They are companions that hunger for him. Maybe he has made this supreme effort of waiting for the grape harvest so he could be there, lying in the doctor's office, waiting for the moment when the kitchen door will open again, and the doctor will come back with some new wine for him to taste.

As always in these cases, there's an exchange. Into the kitchen waft the smells of bandages, of iodine, the smells of pain meeting the other smells. The asphyxiating ether swirls around for a moment, gains ground, then slinks away, apparently dethroned by the browning onions, driven back by the smell of goose fat. The absolute delight of sizzling bacon, and the patient will remember only that smell and the taste of the new wine.

And the glass of must that the doctor brings him, his large frame filling the open door, makes him drunk.

For an instant, he had glimpsed the young woman with the sweet smile, the young wife of the man who will accompany him to the end, who will keep talking to him about grape harvests, young Agathe with the white embroidered dress, he recognized her voice. She speaks quietly, bustles about, leans down, stands up, moves off, disappears.

He would have liked to call to her, to have her come over, to see her as something other than a friendly shape.

Too late, and now the new wine sends him violently down. He sinks deeper and deeper, feeling both light and very heavy. He won't die of his terminal disease, but of a hangover.

Another evening, another patient is waiting for the doctor who is so patient.

It's hard to keep fighting, pulling bodies toward the light, when they themselves sometimes plunge into night.

The dying light hits the pane of frosted glass, the window faces due west. Mouth wide open, the patient swallows the last ray of the setting sun.

Water in the plain dotted with poplars.

Flood season has returned, the water of the river has overtopped the dikes along the Garonne, but it won't reach the church courtyard. There was no point in carrying the furniture upstairs. The children are sorry not to be going to school by boat.

And as always, early in the evening in the doctor's house, in all seasons, a straggling patient arrives, either for a small illness or also for the other one. There is no middle ground between these moments of the waning day, we come only for the two extremes, for the greatest suffering that becomes heightened as night approaches, and also for the slight anxiety, that unease of the small evening of the soul, when sight begins to fade.

So we hurry to see the one who will keep the darkness at bay for a few moments more. We need reassurance when evening falls.

Translated by William Rodarmor

The Master of Manners

Henri Duvernois

AS SOON AS JUSTINIEN CELTIBÈRE decided to get engaged, he went to announce the news to Mme des Roches, his elderly aunt, who invited him to lunch.

"What is your fiancée like?" she inquired.

"My fiancée, dear Aunt, was marvelously brought up in England. She's very kind to me. But I must admit that there are moments when it seems I may be offending certain sensibilities of hers that I'm simply unaware of—it's just a feeling I get. Could you perhaps enlighten me?"

HENRI DUVERNOIS (1875–1937) began his literary career as a Parisian journalist and soon became a celebrated short story writer. His stories, published weekly in newspapers, were later collected in volumes such as *Les Marchandes d'oubli*, *Fifi-noiseau*, *Le Chien qui parle*, and *La Lune de fiel*. A well-known gourmand, he contributed stories to many food publications as well. He also wrote six novels and a dozen theatrical works— one-act plays and operettas—that enjoyed great popularity in the 1920s and '30s. This story appears in a 1998 anthology edited by Philippe Jost, *La Gourmandise: Les chefs-d'oeuvre de la litté-rature gastronomique de l'Antiquité à nos jours*.

"Come have some lunch."

Old Mme des Roches loved to eat. Her cook prepared her delicacies that she savored with looks of rapture, all the while making refined, elegant gestures with her white hands. Justinien, a simple soul, had a ferocious appetite; he wolfed down three vol-au-vents, a fillet of sole Dugléré, and four lamb chops. His aunt observed him with shock and disdain.

"Listen, Justinien," said Mme des Roches. "Diderot, who was a great wit, was once invited to the home of a noble-woman. She particularly noticed the innumerable mistakes he made in eating his soft-boiled egg."

"So?"

"So, my poor friend: you are not Diderot, but you eat like a pig. I'm sure your fiancée has noticed, and it disgusts her.

"You probably imagine that you've just had lunch. Wrong! You've just *eaten*. And I'm being polite! It would be a waste of time to point out that that you don't sit properly, you clutch your knife and fork, you chew with your mouth open, and—horror of horrors!—you drink as if you were in a wine cellar."

"I'm so sorry!" he exclaimed. "I'm truly mortified."

"Come, now. Here's the remedy: a man named Douglas Walwerton-Lee, an Englishman from the best circles. He's not very rich, but he has admirable manners. I'll send him a note to let him know that you'll drop by tomorrow morning."

The next day, a greatly intrigued young Celtibère stood at the door of a cowshed and rang the bell. He was invited into the barn, at the end of which a crude ladder led to a large, empty whitewashed room, bathed in sunlight. That is where Mr. Douglas Walwerton-Lee, an eccentric and traditionalist, lived with a bathtub, an exercise machine, a saddle of tawny leather, a washstand, and twelve pairs of bootless shoe trees.

"*Bongjoue,*" the master of manners intoned in heavily accented French. "Have a seat on the chair."

With his long, gaunt, closely shaved face and a nightshirt graced by a finely fluted frill, Walwerton-Lee looked like a slight, jovial old lady. He set his terms: twenty pounds sterling for ten sessions—five lunches and five dinners.

"I've trained nastier sorts than you!" he said. "A banker, a truly disgusting fellow, let me tell you. But if you were to see him now, you'd think he was born with knife and fork in his hand!"

On that note, he made them a reservation for one o'clock in a private dining room of the best restaurant in Paris.

Justinien saw his teacher arrive done up in a morning coat that looked impeccable from afar but smelled of mothballs up close, wearing a carnation in his buttonhole and a top hat pushed down to his ears, in proper fashion. The student felt as anxious as a schoolboy standing at the blackboard with a lump in his throat. "I've ordered the courses," chortled Walwerton-Lee, his face split in a silent laugh. "Nothing but difficult ones!"

He first seated his student and made him puff out his chest and turn his head, as if posing in a photo studio. Then he took his cane, unscrewed the handle, and pulled out a little ivory baton, which he laid beside his place setting.

"This way I can tap your fingers when you don't obey, dear old boy."

Lunch began—and what a lunch! It was sheer torture. The meal was copious. Right from the hors d'oeuvres, Celtibère felt crushed by his teacher's superiority, hypnotized by the graceful motions of the man's precise, skillful hands.

"You see, my jaw is discreet—not a sound, nothing moves—whereas your chin is already greasy, dear boy!"

It was the crawfish that did it. Masterfully, the teacher shelled them without using his fingers. Imitating him, Justinien managed just one while his teacher dispatched a dozen. Then there was fowl, foie gras, and asparagus. Celtibère spread the foie gras on his bread and boldly seized the asparagus, which he shredded with his teeth. His knuckles received several sharp raps from the little ivory baton. The master laughed with glee.

"Attention! I shall now show you the proper way to drink Champagne and Saint-Julien (he pronounced them *shom-painya* and *sentyoulee*), as well as Asti Spumante, cognac, and curaçao. Watch carefully. For a fine wine, first I warm it a bit in the palm of my hand, then it goes down the hatch—like this! Napkin. Then I take my knife and fork again, holding them at the very tip. Alas! I forgot the cheese."

The meal lasted three hours and ended with fruit. Walwerton-Lee with an orange was a sight to behold: in mere seconds he'd trimmed off the peel and removed all the seeds.

"I'm tired," said Celtibère. "Anyway, it's late; we'll have coffee next time."

The bill came to two hundred and eight francs. The author of this true story must add that the student was forced to drive his teacher home, as the latter was quite fatigued by the lesson.

"I'm a hardworking soul," groaned Walwerton-Lee as he climbed back into bed. "It bores me so to have nothing to do. I shall give you lessons from morning till night! You eat like a swine, my dear Celtibérien, but you're so sweet! A good boy; a very good boy indeed!"

After five lunches and five dinners in a similar vein, the young man was all set to cut a suitable figure.

Finally, there was a great formal dinner at the home of M. and Mme Charmoise de Hautbut de Puyfer. Mme des Roches was invited to witness her nephew's progress in that art of which Mr. Walwerton-Lee was a past master.

But despite all one's studies, no one is immune to emotion. Thus the rider, so accomplished in the training ring, clings to the mane of a docile horse, and the speaker who confidently delivered the speech to his wife stammers in front of the audience. Justinien's emotions were his undoing.

"You're so stiff," his fiancée Hermance remarked as the soup was served. "Is your neck bothering you?"

Justinien smiled smugly. But Mme des Roches, who incessantly scrutinized him with her lorgnette, was making him nervous. Elbows at his side, knife and fork held elegantly with his fingertips, Justinien struggled with a horrible piece of lobster that finally slid across his plate and went flying. It landed three feet away, right on the dress of an incensed fat lady, after triggering a shower of sauce and spattering his blond fiancée. Panic-stricken, Justinien thought he could see Mr. Walwerton-Lee's silent laughter on all the guests' lips. He anxiously gulped down a glass of Pommard, which produced a coughing fit that sent the wine squirting out his nose.

"Whatever is the matter with you?" Hermance whispered. "You're usually so deft."

Justinien felt greatly relieved to be back in the living room with his fiancée.

"Don't you think that getting together to eat," he asked, "is a vestige of savagery?"

At that instant, one of the guests, a Monsieur Leglenthyère, broke in. *"How do you do, old fellow?"* he said.

"Why are you speaking to me in English?" Justinien asked nervously.

"Because I know everything. I met Walwerton-Lee this morning, and he told me he was giving you lessons. I imagine they couldn't be math lessons, but English! He told me you were doing very well, and he was quite pleased with you. 'Watch him carefully tonight,' he said to me. 'You'll be amazed!'"

Translated by Rose Vekony

The Plate Raider

Thanh-Van Tran-Nhut

EVEN WHEN HE WAS VERY LITTLE, Ernest Pardieu knew something wasn't right: his purée would be both thin and lumpy, carrots crumbled under his fork, and his steak was something a shoemaker might use.

Because she was either stingy or unskilled, his mother overcooked food or didn't salt it enough, and she avoided spices as if they were the work of the devil.

So as not to waste away completely, little Ernest developed the salutary habit of showing up—seemingly by accident—at his chubbiest classmates' houses just before dinnertime. An invitation to stay was inevitably extended

THANH-VAN TRAN-NHUT (1962–) was born in Vietnam, studied in the United States, and lives and works in France. She is a mechanical engineer, a tireless traveler, and the author of the popular "Mandarin Tân" series. In books like *Le Banquet de la Licorne* (2009), *Les Travers du Docteur Porc* (2007), and *Le Temple de la grue écarlate* (1999), Tân pursues crimes and good food in seventeenth-century Vietnam. This story is from her 2009 collection *Le Palais du Mandarin*.

and never refused. Like a member of the family, Ernest enjoyed tender, juicy roasts cooked by *cordon bleu* mothers. He boldly eviscerated stuffed tomatoes, releasing juices redolent of shallot and saffron. He savored glazed slices of apple pie studded with raisins.

At the age of ten, with his considerable but still amateur savoir-faire, young Ernest Pardieu chose his goal in life: he would be a professional plate raider.

He found ways to crash birthday and tea parties, where he was just one child among others, but the most gluttonous and voracious of them all. He refined his approach tactics, excelled in the art of infiltration, and stopped eating at his mother's.

As a teenager, he could be found at drunken parties, arriving after the revelers had succumbed to liquor or psychedelics and lay sprawled in battered armchairs, leaving the refrigerator defenseless. Ernest Pardieu would then raid the cubes of fragrant cheese, chips, and dry sausage. He took everything and disdained nothing except peanuts, whose vulgar smell he hated.

As an adult, he swore off his earlier crude manners and lapses of taste, though he wasn't above stealing the occasional pacifier from an unsupervised baby.

Pardieu began to pay careful attention to his appearance, usually dressing in black and parting his hair on the side. At book launchings, he would casually lean on the display stand of a publisher whose works he had no intention of reading, stretch a practiced hand over a tray of petits fours, and eat them with an air of put-upon disillusionment. In fact, each mouthful was a little delight: the puff pastry sparkled when he bit into it, the zigzags of icing fired off bursts of coffee and chocolate, the little cream puffs exploded with sumptuous spurts of confectioner's custard. Far from anchoring himself to a booth, Pardieu flitted from flower to flower, excited by the variety of foods available. He relieved a Breton publisher of a miniature vol-au-vent garnished with bits of scallop and seasoned with a drop of apple *pommeau*. At a Provençal colleague's, he nibbled at tomato confit mille-feuilles. At the booth of a national newspaper he savored rabbit rillettes in apricot jam and curried tandoori mussels served in little tasting spoons with curved handles. He elegantly downed oysters in lemongrass gelée, smoked salmon with guacamole, and green tea mousses. To mislead overly sharp-eyed waiters, he would occasionally say in a friendly voice to nobody in particular:

"Would you like me to bring you a few tasting spoons?"

Then, with a magnanimous gesture, he would scoop up a half dozen, and go off to eat them in peace.

Pardieu liked book parties, but he loved gallery openings, where he would mingle with the early crowd. He had a weakness for *verrines,* those little glasses full of marvelous layered ingredients, as delicate as jewels. He liked veloutés of avocado and shrimp brightened with a sprig of watercress, and chiffonades of Parma ham with slivers of melon, which were tiny gold and garnet gems. To fit in, he would take a verrine of four-spiced foie gras with crushed pear drizzled with honey and go stand in front of a painting chosen at random. There, he would nod a few times, step back, mutter something, lean closer to the work in question. This required hardly any effort and allowed him to savor the subtleties of the culinary creation at leisure.

If someone asked his opinion, he would pretend to only

speak only Hungarian. If someone asked for his card, he produced an ivory business card in the name of Zoltán Kosztolányi, a correspondent for *Magyar Posta,* an art magazine. This satisfied everyone and left the cosmopolitan plate raider a free field.

No doubt about it, it was a good life. Thanks to his talent, Ernest Pardieu had blossomed into a high-class parasite, on intimate terms with luxury and pleasure without having to open his wallet.

Just the same, he didn't want to be thought uncultured. To enhance his intellect, he spent time at both the Sorbonne and the Collège de France. Not to take classes, but to attend doctoral thesis defenses. These had two advantages: they presented the results of arduous research, and were followed by very pleasant cocktail parties.

True, he did have to sit through a few dry sessions. One involved the asymptotic analysis of layer limits in fluid mechanics, another an experimental study of the function of anaphoric marks of textual cohesion in linguistics. But overall he was rarely bored, and during a physics defense he even learned that quarks have flavors.

Pardieu didn't choose the theses randomly. He came only when the doctoral candidate had a name from southwest France, which practically guaranteed a cocktail party with matchless delights. Thus, after a sociology defense that was especially hard to swallow, he was able to sample canapés of capered ringdove breast whose flavor he remembered long afterward. On another occasion he stuffed himself from a *dodine* of wild quail, followed by peppered pine nuts in dark chocolate.

Leaning against the walls of these venerable institutions, holding his little plate, Pardieu considered himself an accomplished humanist, who filled his belly only after having fed his brain.

One fall day, feeling a pang of hunger, he noticed a funeral party that was ending. A certain Monsieur Chanzy had just been buried, with a very well-dressed crowd in attendance. Trusting his instinct, Pardieu fell in behind a woman wearing an otter stole and mingled with the funeral party, which was heading for the late Chanzy's penultimate residence for a farewell buffet.

In the reception hallway, a long table set for a royal feast immediately caught Pardieu's eye. There was a profusion of dishes, from a salad of liver fried with truffles to a lobster chartreuse with chanterelles, by way of spiced roast pigeons. A cargolade of *petit-gris* snails stood next to an oyster tartare that smelled of Provence *garrigue*. A crème brûlée with chestnut preserves waited near macaroons stuffed with red fruit and cocoa-covered semolina cookies with *reinette* apple preserves. His appetite heightened by the rich smells and exotic aromas, Pardieu could hardly contain his joy. He waited impatiently for some hungry guest to give the signal to go on the attack.

As it happened, Ms. Otter Stole made the first move, wolfing down a guinea fowl ravioli. Pardieu promptly took a crab canapé. Otter Stole seized a tuna zucchini roulade. Pardieu countered with a snail flan in parsley cream.

Meanwhile, the other mourners were sharing vivid anecdotes about the dead man, stressing his wisdom and praising his sense of humor. Just as Pardieu was about to swallow a frogs' legs fricassee in a hazelnut croûte, they turned to him so he could say a few words. He looked down and spoke in a choked voice.

"My memories of Monsieur Chanzy so far transcend words, I am reduced to silence."

The assembly found this delicate sentiment very moving, and went on to the next person, who spoke about the deceased's exemplary career:

"Augustin Chanzy was not only a man with a big heart, he was also an unrivaled researcher, a renowned scientist who will influence generations to come."

Finally free, Pardieu went back to enjoying the frogs' legs. He picked up a piece of the golden crust and greedily lifted it to his lips while the panegyric dragged on.

"Let us salute Augustin Chanzy for his research on the eradication of the *hymenolepis* tapeworm . . ."

"Tell me about it," muttered Pardieu, taking a deliciously crunchy mouthful.

This turned out to be a mistake, because he immediately detected the hated taste of roasted peanuts. In revulsion, his body tried to expel them in a sneeze, but Pardieu violently repressed it, so as not to attract attention. As a result two large peanuts shot up into his sinuses and lodged in his nasal cavities. With these blocked, he was now in danger of suffocating. He tried to open his mouth to breathe but the soft caramel oozing from the croustade glued his teeth together and kept any air from entering.

In this way, his nose plugged and his lips tragically sealed, Ernest Pardieu died in the exercise of his duties at the very moment that the funeral oration for his host concluded:

"To the memory of Professor Chanzy, our late director of the Department of Parasitology."

Translated by William Rodarmor

Belle du Seigneur

Albert Cohen

AT TEN MINUTES TO SEVEN, the three Deumes took their places in the drawing room, grave-faced and dignified. When she had sat down, exuding mothballs, her cheeks aflame with the lavender water she had rubbed into them, Madame Deume declared that since their guest was not due to arrive for forty minutes, at seven thirty, they should make the most of the time to put their feet up, sit back in their

---

ALBERT COHEN (1895–1981) was a Swiss novelist who wrote in French. He worked as a civil servant for such organizations as the International Labor Organization. He was born in Greece of a Sephardic Jewish family and became a Swiss citizen in 1919. Considered his masterpiece, his popular novel *Belle du Seigneur* (1968) won the Grand Prix du roman from the Académie française. It was translated under the same title by David Coward in 1995.

In this excerpt from chapter 19, Antoinette and Hippolyte Deume and their son Adrien (called "Didi") nervously await the arrival of an exalted dinner guest: Adrien's boss at the League of Nations.

---

armchairs and relax, closing their eyes if they could. But these words of wise counsel were soon forgotten in a welter of nervous to-ings and fro-ings and brittle smiles.

There was a great deal of sitting down and standing up. Severally they got up to move the table a wee bit closer, to open the plush curtains just a trifle wider, to push back a coffee table, to rearrange the liqueur bottles by size, to put the curtains back as they were because they were far, far better like that, to check if that was really a spot down there or just a shadow, to move an ashtray, to make more of the display of the cigar and cigarette boxes, for Adrien had an eye for creative disorder which he strove constantly to refine with the aid of his limited edition deluxe art books.

For her part, Madame Deume left the room seven times: to give orders to "the domestics"; to make sure the hall did not smell of *potage bisque*; to dab a little more powder on her face; to cast a final look over the dining-room table and the downstairs lavatory; to straighten her choker; to remove any excess powder and smooth her eyebrows; and, finally, to take that last-minute precaution which was followed by the clank of the cistern and the rushing of mighty waters. When she returned, slapping her hand over her hindquarters, she advised both Hippolyte and Didi to follow her example, one after the other.

"What does your watch say?" she asked for the third time.

"Seven thirteen," said Adrien.

"Another seventeen minutes," said Monsieur Deume, who went on reciting to himself pieces of advice from his etiquette book.

"Didi, it is the case, is it not, that your wife will come down the moment he gets here?"

"Oh yes, Mummy, I've told Martha exactly what she's to do. She'll go up and call her the minute he arrives."

"Talking of Martha," said Madame Deume, "it will be her job to answer the door, I've just been to tell her."

"But why not the butler? It would be much smarter."

"He'll see the butler soon enough since the butler will be serving dinner. But I also want him to have sight of the maid, housemaid rather, I'll get her to wear the little embroidered apron and white cap I bought for her yesterday. Seeing as how we've got a housemaid and butler we might as well show them off. I've told Martha exactly what to do, how to open the door, how to say good evening, how to take his hat, how to show him into the drawing room where we'll be waiting. (Monsieur Deume gave a shudder.) I also bought her a pair of white cotton gloves, like the ones at Madame Ventradour's. I've already told her to put them on, so that she doesn't forget them at the last moment. She's such a scatterbrain. So, barring accidents, which can never be ruled out, everything is well in hand."

"Listen, Mummy, I've had a thought," said Adrien, who stopped his pacing and stood, hands in pockets. "There's something been bothering me: the hall, it looks rather bare. That abstract painting in my bedroom, I think I'll fetch it down and put it in the hall. It was done by an artist who's all the rage just now. It'll go well there instead of that engraving, which doesn't amount to anything much."

"But Didi, there's no time!"

"It's all right, it's exactly twenty past seven. It's not going to take me ten minutes to do it."

"But what if he gets here early?"

"Higher-ups never arrive early. Come on!"

"But at least I won't have you carrying that picture yourself, it's far too heavy. It's a job for Martha."

At seven twenty-four, perched on a stool which had been placed on a chair, Martha was attempting to hang the picture, which positively churned with spirals and circles, while Madame Deume held her firmly by her thick ankles.

"Careful you don't fall!" shouted Monsieur Deume.

"What's the matter with you, yelling like that?" asked Madame Deume without turning round.

"Sorry I'm sure," said Monsieur Deume, who didn't dare admit that he was merely getting his socially acceptable raised tone of voice in trim.

At seven twenty-seven, as the picture was finally hung, the doorbell rang and Madame Deume gave a sudden start which sent Martha tumbling off her perch, while further down the hallway a voice bellowed: it was the exchange angrily informing the subscriber that the phone had been left off the hook. As Monsieur Deume helped up Martha, whose nose was bleeding, Adrien hurriedly put the chair and stool back where they belonged, the doorbell jangled impatiently, the phone brayed, and, in the kitchen, the butler and the caterer's man from Rossi's split their sides.

"You see! He did come early!" whispered Madame Deume. "Wipe your nose, you silly creature, it's bleeding!" she muttered to Martha who, panic-stricken, reeled round and round and snorted blood noisily into the handkerchief which was held out to her. "There! That'll do, it's stopped bleeding. Go and change your apron, and be quick, it's got blood all over it! Get another apron! Smile! Apologize for the delay! Say you had a little accident! Smile, girl, smile!"

The three Deumes scurried into the drawing room,

closed the door, and stood motionless, hearts thumping, forcing a steadfast smile, already shaping for the gracious welcome. "You and your last-minute ideas about changing the pictures," muttered Madame Deume. This said, she refashioned her smile to cover her fury. The door opened but it was only Martha, apron askew, who said "It's the bomb, mum." Madame Deume let out a "Phew!" But of course, the *bombe glacée*! She had forgotten all about it.

"Are you waiting to take root, you stupid girl? Get along with you, and wash your face! And put your apron straight! Give me back my handkerchief! On second thought put it with the dirty washing, not in the bin, put it in the bag with the fine things! Go on, and comb your hair! As for you, Adrien, wanting to hang up pictures at the last moment, well, I just can't think what got into you! Still, it could have been worse. Let's hope she doesn't manage to break a leg. All we need now is for that girl to have an accident and we'd be saddled with her hospital bills. What's the time?"

"Seven twenty-nine."

"One minute to go," said Monsieur Deume in a constricted voice.

Madame Deume ran her eyes over her two men. Had they dirtied their clothes in the excitement? No, thank the Lord.

Monsieur Deume was chewing the cud of fear. He was sure he'd make a mess of saying how delighted he was when Adrien introduced him.

All three of them went on just standing there, not having the courage to sit down and behave normally. They waited in silence, awkward under a veneer of ease. The minutes ticked by but the smiles stayed put. Eventually Madame Deume asked what time it was.

"Thirty-nine minutes past," answered Adrien. "When he rings," he added, rigid with tension, in a voice barely audible through lips which hardly moved, "I shall count to fifteen to give Martha time to open the door and take his hat. Then I'll go and greet him in the hallway, it's more friendly. You two can stay here in the drawing room."

"You must introduce me first. The hostess is generally supposed to take precedency," whispered Madame Deume in a stiff-backed, starched undertone.

"Why on earth do you want him to introduce you?" breathed Monsieur Deume, no less rigid, with only his lips moving. "You know he's Monsieur Solal because we're waiting for him. We've been talking of nobody else for the past month."

"What's the time now?" asked Madame Deume without condescending to reply.

"Seventeen minutes to eight," said Adrien.

"I make it sixteen," said Monsieur Deume.

"I set my watch by the radio," said Adrien.

He raised his hand and cocked an ear. The distant sound of an approaching car grew louder and rose above the sigh of the wind in the poplars. "This is it," breathed Monsieur Deume in a strangled voice which would have been more at home in a dentist's chair immediately prior to an extraction. But the car did not stop. Erect, their ears straining, studying each and every sound from outside, the three Deumes waited bravely on.

"It's the proper thing to arrive a little late," said Madame Deume. "What's the time?"

"Eleven minutes to," replied Adrien.

"Oh yes," she went on, "people with manners always

arrive a little late, in case the hosts aren't quite ready. It's a mark of thoughtfulness, of consideration for others. Quite different than the hoi polloi."

All three remained on their feet, waiting in an aspic of beaming, dismal refinement.

Speechlessly slumped in their armchairs, they looked weary and listless. Monsieur Deume hummed inaudibly in an effort to appear natural. Adrien's right shoe, its toe perpendicular to the floor, trembled uncontrollably. With lowered eyes, Madame Deume inspected her long, squared-off fingernails, each with an unsightly five-millimeter white crescent inscribed by the penknife she had cleaned them with.

"How's the time going?" she inquired.

"Ten minutes past eight," said Adrien.

"I make it eleven minutes past," said Monsieur Deume.

"I told you, I set my watch by the radio," said Adrien.

"You're quite sure he said seven thirty?" asked Madame Deume.

"Yes, but he did mention he might be a little late," lied Adrien.

"I see, well that's something. Still, you might have told me."

They resumed their waiting, feeling humiliated but hiding their discomfiture from each other. At twenty-three minutes past eight Adrien looked up suddenly and raised one hand. A car door slammed.

"This time it's him," said Monsieur Deume.

"On your feet!" ordered Madame Deume, who, as she got up, smoothed herself down behind for one last check. "Don't forget to introduce me first."

A ring at the door. With a premature smile, Adrien straightened his tie and began counting, waiting till he got to fifteen before emerging to greet his glorious guest. He had got to twelve when a perspiring Martha, looking guilt-stricken, entered and announced to the trio of statues that it was a man for next door who'd got the wrong house.

"Send him packing," said Madame Deume, now completely flustered.

When the maid had gone, all three looked at each other. Forestalling the question which was waiting in the wings, Adrien said it was almost eight twenty-five. He whistled under his breath for a moment then lit a cigarette, which he stubbed out immediately. More cars went by, but not one of them stopped.

"Something must have gone wrong," said Monsieur Deume.

Madame Deume fingered her lump for a moment. Then she said: "Adrien, go and phone him at the Palais. An hour late! It's really too much, I don't care if he is an important dignitary."

"He won't be at the Palais at this time of night. We'd be better advised trying to reach him at his hotel."

"Well, go and phone his hotel then, if that's where he lives," said Madame Deume, and she added a quick intake of breath which signified that she found it very peculiar that such an important man should not have a home of his own.

"It's a bit awkward," said Adrien.

Right! If the menfolk didn't have the stomach for it, she most certainly did! Trailing a strong whiff of mothballs in her wake, she stepped out decisively and headed for the telephone in the hall. For the entire duration of her conversation the two men stood quite still, saying nothing. Monsieur Deume stuck his fingers in his ears, so ashamed did he feel. For her return, Madame Deume wore an expression of considerable self-importance.

"Well?" asked Adrien.

"You're such a scatterbrain, Adrien Deume," she said in a tone which was almost good-humored. "It was all a terrible misunderstanding. He said that you'd invited him for next Friday! All this trouble I've gone to for nothing! But he said he'll call round at ten, after an important dinner he has to attend, just as soon as he can get away, which is very decent of him, because it's bound to upset his plans. Really, Adrien, I cannot understand how you could be so careless!"

He did not argue, but he was not taken in. The Under-Secretary-General's excuse was so thin it was transparent. Why only the day before yesterday he had left a note for Miss Wilson to give to the USG to jog his memory about the dinner party tonight, a reminder, he'd only done what the Hellers did. Fortunately he hadn't mentioned it to Mummy. The USG had forgotten, that was all. Yes, say nothing, it was much better to be thought absent-minded than to be classed as the sort of chap whose dinner invitations get forgotten. Pity, though, about the two hundred grams of caviar, especially since it was fresh. But he was coming, that was the main thing.

"Did you speak to him personally?" he asked.

"I got a valet first," said Madame Deume with reverence, "then I was put through to the Under-Secretary-General himself. He was quite charming, I must say, such a pleasant voice, very resonant, with a hint of depth to it, and so polite! To begin with we untangled the misunderstanding, then he made his apologies and said how very sorry he was, he put it so well, I mean, perfect savoir faire. It was a good thing I thought of telephoning when I did because I only just caught him, he was about to leave to go to an important function."

"Is that what he said?" asked Adrien.

"Well I imagine it's an important function, since it's being given by the Argentinian delegation. Anyway, he said he'd make his excuses to the delegation, explaining about the misunderstanding, and he'd leave the moment dinner was over and come on to us. Really, charming beyond words! He quite won me over, and I don't mind admitting it! Besides, we should appreciate all the trouble he's putting himself to, I mean it's extremely good of him to come on here immediately after dining with members of the Argentinian government, it's awfully flattering for us. It's funny but I felt completely at my ease when I was chatting with him. I think I can say that we already know each other," she concluded chastely.

"Sounds as if Argentinians have dinner rather late," said Monsieur Deume, who was starving.

"The more formal the function, the later dinner is served," said Madame Deume, the milk of her charity having been set flowing by her phone call. "At least now we know how we stand, and it's a weight off my mind I can tell you. Everything is straightforward now, all cut and dried: he said he'd get here at ten on the dot. Now the first thing on the agenda is to get rid of that butler, I don't want to see his face here anymore, we'll get Martha to lay on a light refreshment. Hippolyte, go and tell that bumptious little upstart that dinner has been canceled. Better tell the caterer's man too. Give them something so there won't be any unpleasantness,

three francs apiece is more than enough, what with everything. Didi'll pay you back."

"I daren't!"

"I'll go," said Adrien, "and while I'm about it I'll let Ariane know what's happened."

"Poor Didi! you seem to get all the nasty jobs. Still, you
are the man of the house. Oh, and send Martha to me in the
dining room, would you, please?"

Following his wife into the dining room, Monsieur Deume
stared open-mouthed at the sumptuously laid table brave
with flowers, candles and champagne. He caught a whiff of
imminent bliss. They'd be able to tuck into a whole feast of
good things and it would be just family, with no important
guest there to keep an eye on them. And they could eat the
asparagus without having to use tongs! His great round eyes
watered at the prospect, and he rubbed his hands.

"Shall we sit down now?"

"I should think not," said Madame Deume. "We'll have a
bite to eat standing up, on the hoof. Martha, you can bring
bread and cheese and the three ham sandwiches left over
from lunch. Put it all in the sideboard and then you can start
clearing away the table things. Come on, girl, get a move on.
For now, just put everything in the kitchen. It will all need
to be put away properly but I'll come along later and show
you exactly what to do, and be careful with my tablecloth,
fold it properly so that it doesn't crease. The dinner will do
for the younger Rampals," she said, turning to her husband.
"I'll phone them in the morning, first thing."

"How do you mean, the Rampals? They're not in Geneva,
are they?"

"Oh dear, what with everything that's been going on, I forgot to tell you. They phoned this afternoon to say they'd just arrived. As delightful as ever. I yearned to invite them then and there to come to dinner this evening. It seemed too good an opportunity to miss, and we could have made the most of the food we'd got in and at the same time it would have shown the Under-Secretary-General the sort of people we know."

"Are they staying long?"

"Three or four days. They're here, you know, for the usual business. I mean they have no choice, given all those disgraceful taxes they're forced to pay in France. She mentioned it ever so amusingly on the phone. She said she'd end up with corns on her hands from all that snipping! You look as if you don't understand, but it's really quite simple, it was a reference to cutting dividend warrants off their bonds. With a pair of scissors, do you see? In those nice little private areas they have in the strongroom at the bank. Anyway, as I was saying when you interrupted, I very much wanted to invite them for this evening, but, since Adrien wasn't in at the time and not knowing what he'd make of it, I didn't dare, because from his point of view he'd probably want to entertain his chief on an intimate basis this first time round, so I was noncommittal, said I'd call them back tomorrow, mentioning I was giving a large, very large, dinner party this evening, there's no harm in them knowing, and didn't know which way to turn what with having to get everything ready. So I'll phone them tomorrow first thing."

"But won't everything have gone all dry by tomorrow, poppet?"

"I'll see to it that it doesn't. With the fridge, there's nothing to worry about. Everything will be just as good when it's warmed up."

"I see," Monsieur Deume murmured unenthusiastically.

"Such a sumptuous menu—and it couldn't have come at a better time, seeing as how the Rampals are nobility," said Madame Deume for the benefit of Martha, who, however, did not register its significance.

"Old French nobility," added Monsieur Deume mechanically.

"Anyway, I'll have a word on this subject with Didi in the morning. I won't bother him tonight, so that he can give all his mind to his boss. If he thinks it would be better to invite his famous Rassets, though personally I've never clapped eyes on them, then he can decide to do that. But either way we shall be hosting a grand dinner party tomorrow night, either for the Rampals or the Rassets, or, failing that, for Madame Ventradour, I say failing that because she's not out of the same drawer, besides all that caviar for a single guest would be a waste. To be honest, I think I prefer the Rassets, it would be an opportunity to make their acquaintance in grand style. Come along, Martha, quick about it, and could we have a little more vim, please? Oh and by the by, Martha, and pay attention to what I'm going to say. The gentleman will be coming at ten, but to be on the safe side I want you in white gloves standing smartly by the door in good time, so you're ready in case he comes early. Go and take up your position by the door at nine thirty. Stand up straight, don't forget your white gloves and mind you don't dirty them, and take good care of your apron too, it has to stay spotless. When the gentleman rings, you open the door with a smile, then you take his hat with a smile, but your smile must not be familiar but modest and . . . servanty. Then, when you've done that, you go to the drawing room, where we'll all be waiting, you open the door and in a clear voice and without smiling this time you announce the Under-Secretary-General of the League of Nations the way it's done at grand receptions. Is that clear?"

"But Antoinette, Adrien said that he would go and meet him in the hall fifteen seconds after the doorbell wings."

"You're right, I'd forgotten. Frankly I prefer it. Announcing guests calls for someone with a certain manner, a certain sense of occasion, a certain knowledge of how things are done. Poor Martha, you wouldn't have been up to it, would you, seeing as how in your lowly station such niceties as receiving important persons do not loom large, I believe! It's not a criticism. It's hardly your fault that you come of humble stock," she ended with one of her luminous smiles.

Adrien returned and said that Ariane was not hungry and would not come down until their guest had arrived. Monsieur Deume made for the sideboard, picked up a small piece of bread, and on it balanced a small piece of Gruyère. "Hippolyte!" said Madame Deume disapprovingly. He didn't need to be told twice, put the bread and the cheese back where he had got them, and stood waiting until his wife had said grace. It was a bit thick, though, saying prayers over a bit of cheese which, to boot, was to be eaten standing up!

"O Lord," began Madame Deume, who parked herself in front of the sideboard with eyes closed, "we thank Thee for granting and preparing with Thine own hands this evening which we are about to spend in the fellowship of the Under-Secretary-General of the League of Nations. Yes, thank you, Lord, thank you. (As she could not think of anything else to say, she repeated "Thank you" several times in a progressively affecting, melting voice to fill the silence while waiting for further inspired words to suggest themselves.) Thank you, thank you, oh thank you. We give Thee thanks too because Thou hast, in Thy wisdom, made the foot of our dear son to lie in the path of his superior. Oh grant that our wondrous companionship here this evening prove to be a plentiful fount of blessings upon our dear Adrien, and may he ever find his path strewn with opportunities for moral advancement and spiritual enrichment. Amen."

Translated by David Coward

Here They Are How Nice

Annie Saumont

THEY'RE COMING. NOTHING'S READY.

Should have thought (her). Long ago. Should have prepared.

Didn't have time.

Rushes here and there (her). Regrets. Scatters. Chooses. Makes an effort. Decides. Gathers. Piles up. Wipes her hands on her dress.

ANNIE SAUMONT (1927–) is France's best-known contemporary writer of short stories, having written more than two hundred of them. She has also translated many books from English, including *The Catcher in the Rye*. Saumont won the short story Prix Goncourt for *Quelquefois dans les cérémonies* (1981) and the Prix de l'Académie française in 2003 for the whole of her work. Her many collections include *Encore une belle journée* (2010), *Les Croissants du dimanche* (2008), *Koman sa sécri émé?* (2005), and *Je suis pas un camion* (1989, tr. *I'm No Truck*). This story is from *Les voilà quel bonheur* (1993), which won the Renaissance Short Story Prize.

Sweep
Open the window
Peel the onions
Pick three red roses in the garden

Nothing's ready. Hums (him), if nothing's ready they won't come back (them).

Wanted them to come (him). Insisted. They're nice. Said so. So what. Takes the clock apart. As if it were urgent.

Could at least (him) help a little. Says clock. Says doesn't care, guests can eat sandwiches.

Says (her) obligations a time for everything. Acrid smell. Roast in the oven? No roast. Damned neighbors burning weeds again.

Crack some nuts
Polish the cutlery
Rinse the stemware
Beat the welcome mat

Hour wheel. Mainspring. Escapement and pivot. Plate. Cleaning. No hurry. Had said (her) stopped running. Had complained. Repairs (him), complains (her). Never satisfied.

Won't take a minute.

Knead the dough
Gently iron the rayon table runner
Keep in the fridge
Put on the plates with a sprig of parsley

Time disappeared, no more machine to measure time parts are lined up on the table. Meditates (him). Gets irritated (her). Damn neighbor's damn dog barking.

Listens (him). Listens (her).

Frown. Dog stops.

Listen some more (him her).

Time suspended.

They're coming. Friendly, will say, how pretty nice view of the countryside. Will say (him) careful, don't lean there. Tiny screws don't touch don't bump. Part lost even one no more clock. No more time. To lose. To gain.

Line a Pyrex mold
Fold the laundry
Whip the cream
Change the canaries' water

Had said (him) would be so much fun. Nothing fancy. Just friends. Now says couldn't have known. Or predicted that the clock. Mechanism seized. If clock in pieces time stopped won't come. Or not until time running again.

Nothing's ready. Missing this and that. Send (her) Josette to the co-op. Call Josette back to give her basket, purse with big bill. Says (her) she was leaving (Josette) empty-handed again. Young people today, no brain. For what we pay them. Plus benefits. What times.

Modern times.

Thinks (him). No reason why it shouldn't work. Perfectly logical. Reproduction antique clock. Made in Japan, Movement guaranteed.

Grate some celeriac
Wipe down the dessert cart
Take out the cheese board and glass lid
Raise the blinds

Not back yet (Josette). Missing mustard and five-grain cereal.

Missing small cogwheel, must have fallen. Move cupboard. Impossible, fragile knick-knacks. They're coming (them) nothing's ready. Not back from the co-op (Josette).

What time? (her) Doesn't answer (him). Since still on errands (Josette) not as late as all that.

Let's hope so.

Says (him) that time, measuring time has always fascinated human beings. Emotional time, biological time, clock time. A time for everything.

Good time had by all (her). Party time. Time is money. Chuckles (him). Ah, women (him again).

Always think that.

Don't understand anything, mix up.

Bring the fruit basket
Don't break the fake Sèvres vase
Mash the artichoke hearts
Polish the patent-leather court shoes

Son of damned neighbor comes to ask for her (Josette). No Josette. Gone to the market. Normal. Housekeeper. Son of damned neighbor works gas company clearly in love with Josette. No reason to be jealous (him).

Not back yet. Therefore in an accident. Run over (Josette) by vegetable truck. Crushed by galloping horse. Smashed disfigured. Raped gutted by butcher in heat. Hanging from meat hook.

Be here soon. White tablecloth. Bottles. Clock fixed. Running a bit fast, not adjusted right. Says (her) that it really could have waited. Tick.

Dreams (him). Would take her (her) in his arms. Would say that all this—table and place settings, fish with sorrel, fried potatoes, veal Orloff side dish—all this really of no interest. Tock.

Will come in (Josette). Empty the basket. Put the change in the drawer. Say that if hadn't been sent shopping would have done everything nothing's ready.

Or will never come back.

Check the weather report
Tip the halogen spotlight up
Pluck the dead leaves off the ficus
Carefully grate the radishes

Times are hard. Fear, anxiety (her). Neighborhood cats. Sinister meowing. On and on. Clock ticking gets on nerves. Inexorable passage of time. One swallow doesn't make a spring.

Wants to kiss her (him). Later darling (her). After all (him) if Josette dead life simpler. Get close again (him her). Like before. Happy days. Would dry the dishes (him). Would mow the lawn. Brrrmmm. Damned neighbor furious, not the time to.

Would find her beautiful, would say so (him). Much more beautiful than grouchy neighbor lady, than seductive Josette. Much more beautiful much nicer. Than. Less. More. Comparing (him).

Repairing (him). Preparing (her).

Lost time is gone forever.

Won't come (them). Too late. Too bad so much the better.

Still rushes here and there (her). Sets crackers on the table.

Trim the hedge
Put out slippers in the entryway
Blend the caper sauce
Shake the cloth

Stops her as she passes (him). Hugs her (him). Against (him). Says that.

Doesn't say anything.

Says that eternal love exists.

Here soon nothing's ready. So happy. Yes both of them. What a joy. Both so much.

Garden gate creaks. Needs oil. Three teaspoons of oil in the salad. Vinegar. A pinch of salt. Door opens door closes. Groceries on kitchen table (Josette). Paella out of the basket. Bought from well-known caterer. Here soon, heat quickly. And strawberry tart. Not crushed (Tart. Josette). Bravo. Wonderful (Josette). A gem. Day off tomorrow. Promise. Tick-tock. Just enjoy how nice.

Here they are.

Translated by William Rodarmor

Cafeteria Wine

Laurent Graff

IT'S A QUARTER PAST TWELVE. You already stopped
working fifteen minutes ago. You're perched on a corner of
your desk, chatting, keeping an eye on your watch, holding
some papers so you will all look busy in case you're interrupted. You aren't paying much attention to what's being
said, you nod vaguely, raise your eyebrows in surprise.
Mainly, you glance around. Time isn't passing. And then
you say, as if amazed, "Hey, it's already half past twelve.
Want to have lunch together?" Actually it's twelve twenty-

LAURENT GRAFF (1968–) is a somewhat mysterious
French writer who reveals very little about himself. He is said
to work as an archivist in publishing, has been influenced by
Buddhism, and—according to a possibly frustrated Spanish
interviewer—does not ride horseback. Says Graff: "As a writer
and a person I am a ghost observer, a secret agent, a stowaway
in life." His books include *Selon toute vraisemblance* (2010), *Il
ne vous reste qu'une photo à prendre* (2010), and *Voyage, voyages*
(2006). This story is from his ironically titled 2001 novel *Les
Jours heureux* (tr. *Happy Days*).

---

five, and of course you're having lunch together, you do
every day, at the same table, with the same people. You get
your jackets and meet in the hallway.

You walk to the cafeteria. It's not far, a bit of a stroll to
whet your appetite. Along the way the conversation becomes
freer, easy. You smile. There are a bunch of you; nobody goes
to the cafeteria alone; solitude is frowned on. Once you're
outside, it's like recess, and you move on to more daring
topics. Françoise is really stacked; Christine has a great pair;
they say that Hélène and Daniel . . . When was the last
time . . . you know, you and your wife? You don't answer
the question; why bother lying, since everybody knows the
truth, to within a day or so?

Choosing your tray. Can't be too careful. The first one,
on top of the pile, is wet; you don't like that. You've got to
show mistrust right away. Really setting our minds at ease
would require a disposable meal kit with a tray and silverware wrapped in cellophane. Fear of germs, fear of the alien.
You take a tray from the middle of the stack. You ignore the
dried egg stain; people behind you are getting impatient.
Let's move on to the silverware, sorted into stainless steel
bins: forks with twisted tines, worn-down knives, teaspoons
with bent handles. First you rummage blindly, then you
refine your choice, eliminating the ones that are dirty or too
banged up, choosing ones from the bottom rather than the
top. Now you have your weapons at last. The daily specials
are written in blue marker on a white board: "Beef stew" and
"Chicken and fries." No fancy language, no honeyed menu-
speak; a spade's a spade. Which is the least risky choice, mad
cow or hormone chicken? Either one will be bad. And even
if it were good, there would still be an aftertaste of the Sen-
egalese cook's black hands in the kitchen—not that you're

a racist or anything, but when it comes to touching food, even when gloved, white hands are more appropriate—or of the sweat of the "Hindu" you once glimpsed through the swinging doors. Maybe you could take two appetizers . . .

"A deviled egg and the chicken with fries," you say. The server is holding a ladle, waiting; people in line are fidgeting. You don't want to seem picky. At least you know what French fries are, and these don't look too greasy. You might have preferred the other chicken thigh, the one next to that one—it seemed more suitable, somehow—but you say thank you anyway. Studying your plate on the tray, the fries piled like pick-up sticks on the chicken, you realize you're hungry after all. You move along obediently, tray against tray. The sliced bread is served in a huge basket with a pair of tongs. Then come the beverages. You're in France, so you're expected to drink wine at meals. As a patriot, this is an order you obey without complaint.

The wine comes in 250-ml bottles, or by the carafe, your choice. You take a sealed bottle. Vin du pays from Hérault, 11.5 percent alcohol, with a picture of grapes on the label. Screw top. There's also a liter bottle, for drunks. The wine has the power to humiliate you. Like truth serum, it scours, strips, reveals. It flows into you like a kind of blood, spreading pain. The soul plunges into it. You grimace as the first swallow announces the metamorphosis. The wine is like a developer solution specially formulated for the wretched misery we stew in. The photograph that emerges isn't a pretty one: a guy sitting in front of his cafeteria tray, head down, grinning at his neighbors' tired jokes, his heart in his mouth.

Translated by William Rodarmor

Paris Dinner

Michèle Gazier

PARISIAN DINNERS ARE CHIC mainly because of their late hour. It's unusual for guests to be expected before nine o'clock, and what with traffic jams and endless aperitifs, you never sit down to eat before ten thirty, a time when our Iberian cousins are just setting the table. Dining too early—and therefore going to sleep too early—hints at recent peasant ancestry. Don't we speak of "going to bed with the chickens"?

Dinner in town, and specifically dinner in Paris, is an institution with its codes—don't arrive early, don't draw attention to yourself—and its customs—bring or have flowers delivered, congratulate the hostess, send thanks the next day. The dinner may bring together people who know, like,

MICHÈLE GAZIER (1964–) was born into a Spanish-Catalan family and turned to writing after working as a translator and as a literary critic for *Libération* and *Télérama*. Her many novels and short story collections include *Le Goût de la lecture* (2010), *La fille* (2010), and *Un soupçon d'indigo* (2008). These two stories are from her 2008 collection *Abécédaire gourmand*.

and want to see each other, but they still won't behave as informally as they might even at a business lunch.

If you are lactose intolerant (no milk, butter, cream, or cheese), dinner can be a trial. A Roquefort tart served as an appetizer can be torture, especially if it's followed by Roman ravioli with cream. In situations like that, the number of guests is critical. The more dining companions you have, the less likely your hostess will wonder about what's on your plate.

Sometimes there will be several of us lactose intolerants around the table. This is an unhoped-for stroke of luck, as sharing allergy stories soon becomes the main topic of conversation. A woman who has done everything possible to hide a phobia that others have called an infirmity since birth suddenly becomes—thanks to a fellow sufferer—the dinner's center of interest. She explains the possible origins of this genetic defect, and everyone finds this so interesting that the fascinated hostess forgets that the evening's lactose intolerants don't have anything to eat.

Some dinners are unforgettable. While not dinners for schmucks, they're dinners for nuts.

It was ten thirty on a weeknight in a beautiful old apartment not far from the Observatoire. Mme de X had gathered a few friends who shared a passion for books and literature. Fifteen guests showed up and introduced themselves. Champagne and whisky flowed like water. The conversation hopped from one subject to another with a lightness buoyed by bubbles and Scotch. The time passed.

One of the guests, a famous writer, leaned toward his neighbor (and reader), a blonde he had just met, and whispered in her ear.

"I'm a little worried. It's already past ten and I'm afraid things are going to turn out the way they did the last time."

"Meaning what?"

"Our hostess forgot to fix dinner, and at midnight we had to seek refuge in the only restaurant that was still willing to take us."

The blonde laughed, stupidly. The writer resumed his conversation with the other guests. The Champagne continued to flow.

Around eleven o'clock, by which time some guests' eyes were already red and glassy, and their tongues somewhat thickened, the convening power majestically rose and announced that she was going to the kitchen to cook dinner. That was all she said. The blonde, a little drunk by now, smiled at her neighbor and whispered that while he may be a very good writer, he was also a terrible gossip. He was laughing with her when the room was suddenly plunged into pitch-black darkness. The fuses had blown—a short circuit in the oven. A few brave souls stuck their noses into the kitchen, and the lights came back, but then went off again, three times in a row.

It was past eleven thirty when a huge dish of raw potatoes and an equally huge blood-red roast descended in the elevator to be cooked in the apartment of the building superintendant, who had been awakened for the occasion. At about twelve thirty, arms laden with hot platters, he rang the doorbell. Madame de X invited her friends to come to the table. Some were snoring, cheek to empty plate. The aroma of the roast wasn't enough to draw them from their deep ethylic sleep—which might be a picture of happiness.

Translated by William Rodarmor

The Dining Car
Michèle Gazier

IT WAS A WINTER MORNING on the Paris-Barcelona
Thalgo train in the early 1980s. I was traveling in a first-class
roomette, which was a crazy indulgence given my modest
budget, but I had long dreamed of taking a trip on this train,
with its deliciously old-fashioned customs. At the platform
at the Gare d'Austerlitz you were greeted by a well-trained
staff, and promptly entered another world, that of stiff, aus-
tere Spain: dark woodwork picked out with copper, benches
covered with tobacco-brown fabric, and that peppery scent
of *Heno de Pravia* eau de toilette that for me will always be
the smell of Spain.

A short, untroubled night. Very early in the morning, as
dawn was breaking behind the lowered curtains, I went to
the dining car for breakfast. The car was almost empty, and
I sat down at a white-skirted table decorated with a wilted
rose in a chrome tube vase. Beyond the window, an urban
landscape of industrial suburbs rolled slowly by, forests of
antennas on roofs and balconies, closed windows, a few with
lights in them. Looking out the wide window gave me the
feeling of being both inside and protected, untouched, and
outside, in air that was probably cold and sharp on this February morning. The low, pale sky seemed to touch the build-

ing rooftops, whose dirty gray concrete looked dredged in some strange powder. It took me a moment to realize that it was snowing, and that those streaks and light patches on the walls were accumulations of snow. I must've shivered, because the waiter asked me if I was cold. I said no, and asked for coffee, orange juice, and croissants.

As I ordered in Spanish, I remembered my first visit to Madrid right after high school. Full of outmoded, bookish knowledge, I asked for *panecillos de media luna*—half-moon rolls, my schoolbook called them. The woman at the bakery burst out laughing when I pointed to the pastry I wanted.

"Ah! Croissannntts!" she said with a smile, and gave me one of those Spanish croissants with their sugar icing.

In the deserted dining car, the silence was almost total. You could barely hear the clinking of the cups and utensils being sorted by the waiter and the silky rush of the train as it gently rocked along the tracks. Outside, the snow looked like cotton.

That breakfast, suspended between two times and places, is unforgettable. The coffee certainly wasn't the best I've ever drunk. It was thick and black, with bluish moiré reflections and a taste of iron. The orange juice came from a bottle in the fridge. And despite a quick visit to the oven to refresh them, the rubbery croissants were sticky, because their icing had melted in the heat. But that morning, in the warm, transparent cocoon of a dining car bound for a still-distant city, sheltered behind a window with a broad view of a landscape that was turning white and hiding its scars with snow, on that morning my breakfast had the taste of happiness, which isn't always that of good things.

Translated by William Rodarmor

The Small Pleasures of Life

Philippe Delerm

HELPING SHELL PEAS

It always happens at that low ebb of the morning when time stands still. The breakfast leftovers have been cleared, the smell of lunch simmering on the stove is still some way off and the kitchen is as calm as a church. Laid out on the waxed tablecloth: a sheet of newspaper, a pile of peas in their pods and a salad bowl.

Somehow you never manage to get in on the start of the operation. You were just passing through the kitchen on your way to the garden, to see if the post had arrived, when . . .

"Is there anything I can do to help?"

As if you didn't already know the answer. Of course you

PHILIPPE DELERM (1950–) is a French sports reporter and the author of some thirty books for adults and children. His collection of short stories *La première gorgée de bière et autres plaisirs minuscules* (1977, tr. *The Small Pleasures of Life*) has sold more than a million copies in France. Here are three of those tiny, delicious pleasures.

---

can help. Just pull up a chair. Soon an invisible metronome will lull you into the cool hypnotic rhythm of shelling peas. The operation itself is deliciously simple. Use your thumb to press down on the seam and the pod instantly opens itself, docile and yielding. For reluctant peas who disguise their youth with shriveled skin, use the nail of your index finger to make an incision that will rip open the green and expose all the moisture and firm flesh beneath. You can send those little balls rolling out at the push of a finger. The last one is unbelievably tiny. Sometimes you can't resist crunching it. It tastes bitter, but fresh as an eleven o'clock kitchen where the water runs cold and the vegetables have just been peeled— nearby, next to the sink, naked carrots glisten on the tea towel where they've been left to dry.

You talk in little snippets of conversation, the words welling up from the calm inside you, and again an invisible music seems to be at play. Occasionally you raise your head at the end of the sentence, to look at the other person; they, of course, keep their head lowered—it's all part of the code.

You talk about work, about plans, about feeling tired— steering clear of anything psychological. Shelling peas isn't a time to explain things, it's a time to go with the flow, in a detached sort of way. You're looking at five minutes' worth of work, but the pleasure lies in rolling up your sleeves and making the moment last, slowing down the morning pod by pod. You plunge your hand into the contents of the salad bowl and let the peas trickle through your fingers. They're delicate as liquid, all those contiguous round shapes in a pea-green sea, and you're actually surprised to discover that your hands aren't wet. A long, fulfilled silence, and then: "Right, all we need now is someone to go out and get the bread . . ."

A CROISSANT IN THE STREET

You were the first to wake. Subtle as a sleuth, you dressed and tiptoed from room to room. A watchmaker couldn't have opened and closed the front door with greater precision. And here you are: outside, in the blue of a morning laced with pink. A tasteless marriage, redeemed only by the purging cold. Each breath produces a cloud of hot air; this early-morning pavement makes you feel liberated and alive. You don't care that the bakery is some way off. Jack Kerouac, with your hands in your pockets, you strike out ahead: each step is a celebration. You surprise yourself by walking on the curb as if you were a child again, as if it were the edge that counted, the boundary of things. This is time in its purest essence, this fragment filched from the day while everyone else is asleep.

Or almost anyone. You're relying, of course, on the warm light of the bakery over there; it's actually neon, but the idea of warmth gives it an amber glow. There has to be just the right amount of condensation on the window as you approach, just the right twinkle in the eye of the baker's wife, reserved exclusively for her first customers. Complicity at daybreak.

"Five croissants, please, and a baguette that's not too crusty."

The baker appears in his floury vest at the back of the shop and greets you as one would a comrade in the hour of combat.

Back outside on the street, you can feel it already: the walk home is never the same. The pavement is less free somehow, the journey more mundane with a baguette tucked under one elbow, a bag of croissants in your hand.

But then you decide to take one of the croissants out of the bag. Still warm and gooey. You indulge in a little gluttony on the move, to combat the cold: as if the heart of the winter morning were crescent-shaped and you were its oven, its haven. Heavy with yellow, you slow down as you encounter the blue, the gray, the fading pink. The best part is already over and the day is just beginning.

POT LUCK

Honestly, it wasn't planned. You still had some work to do for the next day. In fact, you'd only popped over to ask about something, and then it happened:

"How about joining us for a spot of supper? But you'll have to take pot luck."

You relish those few seconds in which you sense the offer coming. It's not just a case of prolonging an enjoyable experience, but of pushing back the barriers of time. The day's been so predictable and the evening looks set to run according to plan. Then, suddenly, within the space of a few seconds, life takes on a new lease: the course of events can be altered, just like that. Of course, you say yes.

Evenings like this are, by their very nature, informal. Not for you a ceremonial aperitif and the sitting-room armchair. In the kitchen, the conversation bubbles away.

"Would you mind giving me a hand with the potatoes?"

Armed with a vegetable peeler, you can talk frankly, without inhibition. You munch a radish, almost one of the family, part of the household. Relaxed. You can move about freely. You've earned the right to poke around in cupboards and hidden nooks. Where did you say you keep your mustard? The mingling smell of parsley and shallots reminds you of another time, a forgotten closeness—those evenings when your homework was spread out on the kitchen table, perhaps?

The words begin to falter. No need to force the flow. Real pleasure lies in appreciating the spaces between. No awkwardness. A library book catches your attention, and you begin to flick through it. Suddenly you hear a voice saying: "I think that's everything." You turn down an aperitif. Right decision. Before you eat, there's still time to chat around the table, your feet resting on the stretcher of a rush-seated chair. As an impromptu guest, you feel free to unwind. The black cat curled up in your lap seems to have adopted you. It's as if life itself had accepted the invitation to take pot luck, and in so doing come to a complete standstill.

Translated by Sarah Ardizzone

Acacia Flowers

Philippe Claudel

MORE THAN ANYTHING, it was a smell that pulled me toward the Sommerviller woods as I was going home from school. That new smell, the smell of the first acacia flowers, was like the call of a siren, like a guard throwing open the gates, a way of entering this season that would be endless, because it would last an entire summer: cops and robbers, dodgeball, haymaking, fishing, evenings under the stars, green wood fires, smoke in your eyes. As soon as I caught that smell, which the evening air, warm and cool at once, greeted with a kind of exuberance, I raced toward

---

PHILIPPE CLAUDEL (1962–) is a French writer, film director, and professor of literature at the University of Nancy. He is best known for his novel *Les Âmes grises* (2003), which won France's Prix Renaudot and Sweden's Martin Beck Award and was shortlisted for the American Gumshoe Award. Claudel wrote and directed the 2008 film *Il y a longtemps que je t'aime* (*I've loved you so long*). This piece appears in a collection of food-related stories published in 2004 by Delphine Montalant, *À Table!*

---

its source. I reached the woods out of breath, looking for the first bunch of flowers among branches still tousled with new leaves. Nostrils flaring and eyes closed, I stood at the foot of the tall, spiky trees, as dazzlingly white as leafy, rustling brides, while the first maybugs, wobbling heavily in their drunken ellipses, brushed my hair and sometimes got tangled in it.

My mother, too, had caught the smell of flowers, honey, sugar, and clear water rising from the streets and houses with their open windows like a vacation in the countryside. Not a word was said; we each knew our roles by heart. I went to collect the clusters of flowers, scraping my knees and legs on the tree trunks, acquiring a crown of thorns on my forehead and my arms, like some skinny Christ. As for my mother, she mixed crêpe batter in an earthenware basin while singing simple, old-time tunes. At her feet, the cat watched for the drops of milk that fell like liquid snow onto the tiled kitchen floor.

I brought home my trembling harvest, its smell seeping into my skin. Mother took the beautiful flowers and gently dipped them in the batter. Suddenly covered with a sad heaviness of syrupy tears, the clusters were then quickly dunked in boiling oil, a bubbling cacophony in the fryer, as if dozens of playful sprites were gossiping without listening to each other and frenetically whispering mysteries in some wordless tongue. This only lasted a minute or two, time enough to spread a rough linen rag on the table where the clusters drained after being pulled from their deadly bath. The cooked batter turned them into delicate golden traceries of a beautiful crackled amber. You blew hard to cool them before sinking your teeth into them, elbows on the table and feet dangling under your chair. Inside the hot batter you found the intact flower, its magic enclosed, a second summer yet to come all contained in the smell and the taste of the acacia beignet.

It was late, my fingers were shiny with oil, my eyelids already drooping toward that cloudless country of innocent sleep. I was a scratched faun, rocked with fatigue, my fingernails black with dirt and my skin already tan. Yawning, I thought of the tall trees, their handsome ornaments, the cracks in their gnarled trunks. Tomorrow I would again go hug and climb them to steal their booty of petals. And my mother would again turn alchemist, as she might again the following day, but not the day after that. Because flowers also die, of course. Like the seasons. Like mothers. And like people, who are merely old children stricken with forgetfulness.

Translated by William Rodarmor

Tears of Laughter

Nadine Ribault

THEY WERE UP IN THE TREES but not moving any more. Occasionally a branch swayed and the sky appeared between leaves that moved a few inches apart, forming minuscule geometric figures in the spaces between them— hexagonal, triangular, square, circular, or octagonal—as if a clever seamstress had taken her scissors and cut up the sky, then tacked little pieces of thick muslin onto a length of blue linen, speckling it with candle wax so it wouldn't fray, and these minuscule white or yellow shapes danced, danced before the birds' exasperated gaze, stood still, danced, stood

---

NADINE RIBAULT (1964–) is the author of the novels *Festina lente* (2000) and *Le Vent et la lumière* (2006), and a number of short story collections, collective works, and translations. "Tears of Laughter" is from her 1999 collection *Un caillou à la mer* (tr. *A Pebble into the Sea*).

In France, the Feast of the Epiphany (*Fête des rois*) is traditionally celebrated on January 6. A cake containing a lucky charm (*fève*) is served, and whoever finds it becomes the king or queen and chooses a partner to wear the second crown.

---

still, danced, a wave of innumerable colored lights that dazzled them completely—a real fireworks display—and made their hearts ache.

Everything suddenly blurred, became diaphanous and tremendously vague, then, at last, the leaves came together again, the branches stopped moving, the air stilled, things found their shape again, and the shadows returned.

The females were still watching the males because for just a moment the light had brought out startling iridescent reflections on their plumage, like violet-eyed peacock feathers, the color of iodine vapor or bouquets of irises.

They had paired up on the highest branches of the oak trees and now and again they fluffed out their downy feathers to twice their normal size. Looking down, their gaze caught the image of pines studded with prickles or of a long table over which a white tablecloth had been thrown, like a bridal veil draped over the wooden surface, a sure sign of festivities to come.

They were silent.

They had already sung a great deal since dawn and they would doubtless sing a great deal more after this brief respite, which was soon to end because, very quickly, the tablecloth had been covered with plates, with knives, forks, and glasses; the table had been surrounded by chairs and the chairs filled with people; and because the air would soon be bringing them something other than simple, inoffensive signs: wilder waves and colder silences.

And that is what happened, suddenly, when there rose toward them a harsh, sharp sound—a cry . . .

"Oh!"

Above the garden, perched on the branches, in the shade

of the oak trees, higher than the pines bordering the terrace, they didn't burst into song again, they waited, heads cocked to one side, and watched down below that speck of sand shivering in the wind—a jellyfish, a sea urchin, a starfish?—a woman laughing so hard she was almost choking.

"I feel sick . . . so sick."

. . . sitting at the long white table, wearing a sleeveless lemon-yellow dress, its low neckline revealing her blue-veined skin.

They took fright: had the sun perhaps fallen to earth, was that not the sun, there, on the verge of dying, sitting at the table, on the marble-paved terrace, after eating and drinking too much . . . ? Then because the warmth of her rays was not as steady, because her eyes were as blue as the sea, because her pulse resounded in their ears and it did indeed seem to them that she was upside down, sitting there below them like that, the seeds of doubt were sown. But in that doubt, which spoiled the harmony of the bright beginning of a summer afternoon, the men rolling up their shirt sleeves and the women bringing out two or three fans, so delicate they were like wisps of fog, in that doubt that descended from the tall trees to rise up in the hearts of all the people gathered around the table—the guests—who had been invited to spend a day in the country, in that doubt a shadow had entwined itself, in the heat of the moment, among all the plates covering the tablecloth, still showing traces of the remains of the meal, surrounded by breadcrumbs—while they all waited, hanging on her expression, waited for her to catch her breath in the center of all the white skin of her lovely, happy face, there was a pebble sliding down her throat, slipping down with a gurgle as if over a riverbed, past the rocks, the shingle, the rushes, along the sand banks—and the birds, up above, had long been eyeing all the breadcrumbs, the last traces of a noisy meal . . .

"Yes I do, I'm absolutely convinced of it! It would still be better to have the Left in power again."

"Oh, how can you say such a thing! What about business? And major public works? You saw where all the money went, didn't you? All those strikes . . . And all the malcontents, all those penniless people who were promised the moon. You really don't know what you're talking about."

. . . ah! for the birds, the breadcrumbs were just so many intoxicating temptations in the midst of all these people's talk, a sight that much more certainly enthralled them, disturbed them, distracted them from their previous questions, to the point of riveting their gaze on the tablecloth's whiteness and the soul of their desires under the blue edges of the plates. They had been under the blue edges of the plates for a long time already. Motionless. Hidden. And the birds were waiting for the end of this endless meal, everyone, even the women and children, were waiting for it to be over so they could get up, stretch their legs, go for a little walk, kick a ball around, have a game of tennis, play with dolls or on the computer . . .

"Grandma Blanche? Grandma Blanche, may I leave the table?"

"In a minute, darling, we're nearly finished, just be patient."

"But Grandma, you know my dollies are hungry!"

"Yes, yes, I know. But dollies' tummies are different from ours, you know. They can wait a bit longer."

. . . you had to be patient, wait a few more minutes—even

if Grandma Blanche was lying, and you knew she was lying, but you mustn't upset her, especially since she was also waiting, like her five grandchildren, waiting for it to be finished, her right hand tucked behind her, between the cushion that had been placed against the back of the chair for her, and her spine, because she had such a bad back!—you had to wait because there was a burst of laughter, a great wave of enthusiasm washing over the table, and above the laughter, meaningful looks were being exchanged, glances meeting, eyes looking away, looking back again, pupils dilated, eyelashes stiff with expectancy, eyes speaking with the passion and warmth of mouths, pairing up for the dance, then letting go, paralyzed, before abruptly meeting again to travel together in the same direction, toward the end of the table.

"Oh, I feel sick . . . I feel so sick!"

. . . where Léa was slicing through the air with her gestures and her interminable laughter.

To hear her, you would think laughing was painful, and each time she laughed, Léa appealed to the Lord, saying her ribs were aching—which Béa couldn't stand, what a drama queen, and all the men, especially Philippe, Léa's husband, was the worst, gaping at her like that. Oh, she would stay free! She would stay free from everything, because she really hated men, without ever having said as much to anyone, she found them unwholesome, lacking in imagination, and hard-hearted, they suppressed their creativity and denied their dreams, yes, she could feel the ties breaking and soon she would sail off alone, she would never use those seductive mannerisms, she would never play that game again, no, not her, never!—yes, Léa was saying that her stomach, her cheeks, her jaws were aching, when her laughter was dying in her throat and she wasn't making a sound, there was just the brilliance of her white teeth, neatly lined up against her glossy pink lipstick.

She raised her hand to her chest.

And yet they had warned her to be careful, it was too hot that afternoon . . .

"Now, Léa . . . You'll make yourself sick!"

. . . but who was it, she had forgotten already, perhaps her father-in-law, who was so attentive, fawning over her, that with a single bat of the long eyelashes framing her pale eyes, she could have gotten him to do whatever she wanted, an advantage she no doubt knew how to exploit.

A sandpiper was running along her ribcage, a tickling that set her off again after each pause, each calming of her laughter, each lessening of intensity, of rhythm so to speak, as if the sea had gone too far out in the great ebb tides and had gotten lost out there, a long way out, in the silence of the night, vanished from sight, unheard, everything would have been lost, even the sound of the waves until it came rushing back, even bigger, louder, more cruel—oh, so much more dangerous than before—it was irresistible, and so poignant besides that Léa found Lise glaring at her from the other end of the table, a look that struck her full in the face, a shock that wounded her at first but which then—strangely— comforted her, accelerated her formidable laughter, and the laugh, suddenly, became a cry that, for the second time, struck the birds in their trees.

"Léa, for heaven's sake, be careful! You're going to make yourself sick!"

Lise! She was so sad that day, of course, and Léa had very nearly forgotten that she found out yesterday that Lise had failed her exam and would have to repeat her year, Lise had explained it to her in the kitchen while she was making the almond biscuits, the apple turnovers, and the sugar tart, Lise wouldn't be seeing Benjamin any more, he was going off to college and she was very worried, she knew their relationship wouldn't survive, it was ending before its time . . . Arms crossed over the long man's shirt she was wearing, she had maintained that it was all over! nothing more to be said! but even so Léa had sensed how sad it made her.

And now Léa was laughing—how dared she?—and Lise, who had seen how quick her moods were, anger, rage, vexation, the feeling that nothing mattered any more, that everything was spoiled, that not one word had mattered of what she'd said and confided that morning, that she'd never, absolutely never been understood, let alone listened to— Lise got up and left the table.

Her wicker chair tipped backward onto the terrace paving stones . . . and stayed there. Just like that. No one thought to lean down and right it, so that after the meal—after everyone had cleared the table, after Lise had gone back to her bedroom, that evening, and after Léa had gone to bed without being able to speak to her—the chair was still lying on the ground because when it fell, almost everyone had been looking at Léa.

Their mother looked across to where Lise had been sitting a few seconds earlier, but as if to verify that, goodness, Lise had left the table once again, it was a habit of hers, a little too passionate and jealous, a little too emotional. She must have gone off to write in her journal or walk in the woods, perhaps even both at once, that was no trouble to her! She took life too seriously, that child, that was all too obvious.

Damn it all! Dear God, don't let her ever leave the country the way she talked about so endlessly. Oh, she would have been so much better off with teaching than all that nonsense she'd gotten into her head. She disturbed her mother's peace of mind. She'd disturbed this wonderful meal too, even though she had every reason to be happy and there were plenty of people far worse off than she was . . . How did the saying go? That's right: little children, little problems, big children, big problems! And ever since she'd turned thirteen or fourteen, Lise had become unbearable. You couldn't do a thing with her anymore. What was her grandfather going to think of such behavior? And it would be she, Emilie, who would be on the receiving end of the lecture:

"I'm telling you, my girl, you'll have to nail her feet to the floor, that little scatterbrain of yours!"

In point of fact, only Blanche's eye lingered on the empty space where Lise had been sitting. With all due respect to her husband, she really loved her granddaughter's enthusiastic spirit and spontaneity. Sadly, in the time it would take her to get up from the table, to move just an inch, Lise would be halfway across the country, energetic, swift and light. In the past, it would have been worth the effort, because she herself was more alert and Lise would have found a pretext for loitering near the house, waiting to be consoled . . . but now, totally self-reliant, expecting nothing from anyone else, Lise roamed the earthen pathways, the lawns, and the sandy walkways. She was probably running away from herself, and the thought of this made Blanche tremble with concern, as she looked at the empty space at the far end of the table— Léa, yet again, had had the marvelous idea of seating her in the middle, she was going to put her neck out of joint from having to turn her head right and left . . . and sweet Jesus, how her back hurt!—anyway, Lise was one of those children who wanted to push back the sky, the earth, and the rivers, needing air, needing to run until she was out of breath, and not to be belittled like this by her sister's unbearably capricious behavior. Blanche noticed it every time . . . Emilie had really spoiled her eldest daughter dreadfully. Everything had been for her benefit, and woe betide anyone who might venture to comment on it, of course . . . even Blanche, her own mother, had never dared. And yet she was very worried about Lise, feeling she was capable of anything, like moving far away . . . oh, no, no, no, so long as she didn't go away . . . it was a good thing she had failed her exam. Given time, she would think things through. She would learn to float above the world so it couldn't touch her.

Then she looked down the table, her gaze moving with astonishing speed to the other end, looking all the way down, passing over the little silvery teaspoons, moving round the Bordeaux bottles and the baguette crusts, the baskets covered with white napkins, sidestepping the remains of the Brie de Meaux, dodging the Champagne glasses, so translucid they were almost invisible, before diving under the fluted edge of the dish where the sugar tart was waiting, so as to avoid the fragility lurking there like a danger, finding tiny grains of brown dust, probably powdered chocolate that had fallen off the truffles Léa had brought out to serve with the coffee—what a dreadful habit, serving the coffee, dessert, and chocolates all at once, everyone knew that at Léa's you drank your coffee cold!—finally her gaze reached her other granddaughter and enveloped Léa so intimately that it divined her thoughts, touching them lightly, instinctively, feeling them vibrate with disturbing disillusionment.

Lise is such an idiot! Léa thought, as she divided up the sugar tart and put small slices onto the plates that Jacques was passing to her.

Oh, blast! There was only just enough to go round. She could never work out the quantities when she was preparing a meal. And afterward, her brother would tell her in private that he was still hungry and swipe a bar of chocolate from the cupboards.

No, Lise hadn't a clue. She was so young and so sentimental. But she would calm down and control her gestures and her moodiness, and if she still wanted to become a botanist and go to Australia "to study the impact of large-scale deforestation on certain species," as she put it, the questions that would come up from being so far away would make her wiser in the end, and Léa hoped she would achieve that.

Love . . . whatever was she thinking?

Oh, the tart was luscious! It had turned out better than the last one.

"Just delicious, my love!" said Emilie, her eyes as round as her mouth.

"Thank you, Maman."

But just barely enough of it, thought Jacques.

No, thought Léa, love is not what makes a woman complete, and it's a good thing Lise and Benjamin hadn't thought of getting married. She was exasperated by all those young people getting married too soon. Living together was a good idea. She would have liked to do that, it would probably have allowed her to feel freer, to live more wildly, to believe she was being swept away by a typhoon . . . probably ... but alas, alas, typhoons only happen far away in Asia, we don't have them here ... we never have ...

"I've got the lucky charm!" she exclaimed.

So on top of everything else, she gets the lucky charm! Béa thought. Really, what should one make of all this? Of this family? Or of certain friendships that had become very important in her life?

Léa put on one of the two cardboard crowns the children had made before the meal—lollipop pink with yellow triangles and green circles—and she got up, walked around the table to the opposite side, and put the second one on Philippe's head.

Well, there it is, thought Béa, the picture of perfect happiness! Trust Léa to come up with this fake celebration of Epiphany with a sugar tart—on the pretext that this year, for the first time, the family hadn't been able to get together for a proper Epiphany celebration—and trust Léa to ask Jacques's children to play along and to laugh about it now. The children had spent the morning with Grandma Blanche, who had tried to explain to them why they would be looking for a lucky charm in a sugar tart ... and in summer, to boot!

"Well!" Jacques was saying to Philippe, "last year at Bray-Dunes his old lady really got on his nerves, kept making a scene because he was paying too much attention to passing miniskirts—know what I mean?—so one day he up and threw her in the drink!"

And Léa's laugh rang out again at her brother's joke— Jacques is such a character, she thought, but he's a bit much sometimes, thought Philippe—and then at the same moment—strange coincidence—everyone noticed that all the birds had stopped singing, a few seconds ago ... Nature had fallen silent, but when, when exactly, no one at the table knew—neither her parents-in-law, yawning from the effects of the wine, nor her grandmother who was straightening Mimi's chair beside her, nor her mother who was pushing breadcrumbs under the edge of her plate, nor her father who was studying the labels on the Bordeaux bottles probably for the tenth time, he must know them by heart, nor her cousin Béa, the Parisian, who was fiddling with her fork—nervously, how surprising—nor Willi, nor her grandfather, nor even Alice who kept studying her nails every five minutes ever since she had given up biting them—no one, absolutely no one, could have said when exactly.

The children had left the table, heading for the tennis court, the bedrooms, the computer, or the television, they had barely managed to wait until the end. Mimi and Lou, as usual, must have walked to the pond to fish for tadpoles and Blanche would soon join them and take them off to hunt for birds' nests in the shrubbery. She knew Léa's charming ways by heart, it was just one big pretense, always had been . . . she usually preferred to show her great-grandchildren the dotted crimson lines on the linnets' eggs or search for a wagtail's nest occupied by murderous little cuckoo babies, naked and blind.

And yet Blanche didn't move that day, she too was waiting for what was clearly to come, the sky was clouding over out to sea in Léa's big eyes and the wind was rising deep within her, near the coast, the fences, the embankments, the jetties, the seawalls, the slabs of concrete she had set up there to hold back the high waves of the equinoctial tides, suddenly unable to resist any more, yes, she could tell from the way the gulls were struggling against the wind, the way the electric poles were swaying dangerously on the slopes of the embankments, from the way the dunes were shifting, from the violet light coming from the depths of the horizon, and especially from the way the fog was rising around the mole at the end of the jetty at the base of the lighthouse, whose light was growing visibly fainter and fainter.

I'm spilling over, thought Léa. Oh, no, I mustn't. I'll keep quiet. I'm laughing. I'm here to laugh. To make them joyful. Carefree. Didn't I bring them together?

The birds in the trees took fright once more when Léa's knife fell onto the terrace paving stones. The metallic sound echoed brutally up to them and made their wings tremble.

Léa's heart swelled like glass expanded by the glassblower's breath, whereas she would have preferred it to be pierced by a sharp instrument to ease it, dilate it, stretch it out in its molten heat so it would ring with a lighter note. But it was just wishful thinking.

. . . She knew that already when she looked up at the single cloud passing in the sky, up above the trees, before she took the crown off and disappeared abruptly beneath the table to pick up the knife—that was something anyway, five seconds' grace—and put it back on the table beside her plate, on the right as always.

Oh, I'm doing acrobatics, she thought, moved to see them all there, watching her pop up from under the table. I'll have to talk to Lise about it, explain to her, to my little Lise, yes, I must find the time to tell her all this before she leaves.

With the movement of Léa's body, the strap of her dress slipped on her shoulder and the beauty mark Philippe knew so well came into view. "We're not going to have any children!" she had said that morning, in bed, when he touched her,

"We're not going to have any children!" and he had focused on that beauty mark while she was speaking, so as not to see her eyes, which were probably full of self-assurance, defiance, and mockery, and because he thought he understood her reasons—or that he needed to pretend to understand them—he had said nothing, added nothing, asked nothing.

A black and yellow butterfly passed close to Léa's shoulder, probably attracted by her gentian perfume—unless it was violet, talcum, or else eau de cologne, it was surprising how different she was every day—at the very moment when Philippe was telling himself it was best to be patient, to wait a little while longer, she would change her mind. In the end, before the butterfly's colored wings caressed the curve of her shoulder, he no longer had the slightest doubt; he had opted for patience and gentleness, while Béa was thinking that there was no one more crass than Jacques, and that his stories were the height of vulgarity, that he really hadn't a clue and that if she kept on spending time with them it would be the end of her. Her mouth tightened at the flood of bitter thoughts, and, catching her grandmother's sympathetic glance, she indicated with her expressive dark eyes that she was praying the meal would soon be over, that these obligations to get together—to share what?—no longer interested her and that she was in a hurry to join her girlfriends so they could go and see *The Wings of Desire* or Pina Bausch or Maguy Mann or Shakespeare or anything at all, Grandma Blanche, anything rather than Léa's posturing, look at that, a permanent performance . . . a real Luxembourg gardens merry-go-round. And Philippe over there, drooling over her, taking off his crown and looking like such a ninny . . . had he no sense of the ridiculous?

To which Blanche replied, with a slight nod of her head, not that she agreed, but that she least understood.

Finally, as happened at the end of every afternoon practically like clockwork, the top of Médéric Grattepanche's head moved along above the top of the garden hedge, telling them that it was now nearly seven and that they would soon have to think about going because there were so many traffic jams in the evenings, with everyone heading back at the end of the weekend. Philippe sat up straighter to get a better view of this nearly bald head just as it disappeared past the corner of the garden. Léa had shivered—he was sure of it—because she was so afraid of this crazy guy who came every month to trim the garden hedges. Médéric Grattepanche had rampaged through his mother's house after she died, and although he told Léa many times that oh, he had smashed up everything at his mother's and Social Services had had to put plastic sheets in the windows, but oh, no, he never broke anything at anyone else's place—and Léa had to make a superhuman effort to understand what he was saying because he had only one tooth left, which barred his mouth like a knife—all the same he had burned the shutters and the doors, broken the floor tiles, torn down the door and window frames, smashed the electricity meters, turned off the water, cut up all the furniture into firewood with a chainsaw, and was living there, his bed a filthy sleeping bag near the fireplace—he loved fire—cooking on a camping stove in an aluminum pot, well then! Médéric Grattepanche might tell her all that, but she was scared stiff of him when he came into the garden and just seeing the top of his bald head passing along the hedges was enough to make her shudder. Several times already, she had wanted him to stop coming—following the example of their neighbors, who had hired someone else from the village, "hedge stealers," Médéric Grattepanche howled each time he went past those people's houses ever since—but Philippe had never given in to her. He continued to employ Médéric Grattepanche despite his wife's reluctance.

That day, however, it didn't stop her from laughing, and although she was obviously trying to hide it, Philippe noticed there was something wrong, she was angry, embarrassed or troubled, when she called to him:

"Next time, Philippe, tell Médéric Grattepanche to cut all the hedges higher, then we won't see him going by anymore!"

And she burst out laughing even more loudly.

Bitch! thought Béa, who didn't like her . . . at all. And Grandma Blanche could go on lecturing her and trying to persuade her to be patient, she wouldn't come again, this was the last time . . . oh yes, today was the last time.

Léa was laughing, showing all her white teeth in a wide smile, her shining eyes fixed on her husband when suddenly—why? she never knew—the plaintive melody of "The Song of the Earth" came into her mind and that made her sad, sad to the point where she couldn't keep up the struggle anymore and it was then, then at that precise moment, that they saw what they had all sensed was going to happen—except Béa, who hadn't seen anything coming at all—thousands of tears pearled at the corners of her eyes, rolled down her cheeks and fell to the corners of her mouth, where they joined her laughter, so clear that a sea urchin was swimming in it, and flowed into her tears, for one second there was no sound—was she choking? the terrified birds wondered, and what a pity for a woman to give herself away like that, thought Béa—and the laughter ceased, and the meal ceased, and everyone stood up—before going home or to their bedrooms—to clear, tidy, wash the dishes, or shake out the tablecloth as Béa now did, in a great and final sweeping gesture.

The breadcrumbs all flew up, then fell back down onto the grass.

Léa went to her room to look for a handkerchief into which she poured the tears that were still in her like the last drops of water at the bottom of a leaky vase. Through the French doors open onto the garden, she listened without moving to the song of the birds that had just begun again, before the start of the wild ballet of the nightjars in the twilight, and before the moon, dressed in a leafy robe, replaced the sun, its reflection glittering on the tadpole pond near which the children had played. A star moved through the water, as the wind blew it, and on the walls of Léa's room—she was now lying between the sheets, not asleep, because she so loved to dream away the evenings, to think about the day gone by without speaking—night's shadows drew their designs: she was a sea urchin on the sand, far away, diverted from her path, a grain of sand over which the sea urchin moved, its body palpitating, its eyes closed, or a drop of sea water moistening the grain of sand on the beach chosen by the sea urchin to stop its race—a moment of repose—in the midst of the village houses, the gardens, courtyards, garages, orchards, woods and in her heart appeared the prickliness of a sea urchin, trembling with memories . . . but which memory, precisely, which memory, in all those beds, in those sheets, those rough blankets and those false silences, among those needles of steel, under those stacked-up chairs and those broken-down cars, those fires of anger, those torn-out windows, all those burned door and window frames, those nauseating odors of plastic, those smashed meters . . . which was hers?

All at once, her consciousness dissolved beneath the sheets, in the blackness of the bed, driven there by the boiling of the amazed blood circulating through her veins at an almost unbearable speed, and this swarming became a trembling, stirring her lips and making her legs twitch, an interminable circling of heat and emotions mixed, a poem being born in her body, illuminating her life, a poem whose words burst into flame as soon as they took shape, and it was a marvel that in this upheaval she could still move so that her hand, beneath the sheets, sought out another hand and pressed it to her. Then she turned over. The brightly colored cardboard crown, which the children had made that morning, fell off the bed where she had put it and rolled on the floor before coming to a stop, dented, at the foot of the dresser.

The tart was delicious.

Pressing her cheek into the pillow and hugging it with her long arms, Léa yawned and yielded to the silence that had collapsed onto her, broken from time to time by the call of a tawny owl far away on the edge of the forest.

The room was bathed in moonlight.

I forgot to pick up Lise's chair, she thought. I'll do it tomorrow. Luckily, Lise isn't leaving until tomorrow. I'll be able to talk to her.

Suddenly there was a shoreline on the walls where sea urchins tried to return to the sea, where birds prevented them from passing, attacking them with their monstrous bodies. She leaped from the boat and sank in the waves, she called, she called for a long time, and no one came. The seaweed no longer existed, it turned into blackberry bushes catching at her dress and scratching at her body. The night was a gigantic object floating above her and pushing her down little by little, minute by minute, second by second, under the water. The sea turned as brown as coffee, rocks were reflected in it and there were gulls, perched on the rocks, looking down at her torn body.

Then quickly the night, the sun, the sea, the waves, the beaches and the shorelines were nothing more than the same solitary child who laughed in her dreams.

"Really . . . ?" she murmured in her sleep. "We aren't going to have any children?"

Outside, at the foot of the trees, not a single breadcrumb remained.

Translated by Jean Anderson

Fast Food

Joseph Incardona

IT MUST BE SOMETHING LIKE TEN YEARS since
we hit the road, Odette and me. One day we just got fed
up with being sedentary types with no kids, boring jobs,
and depressing office parties at the end of the year. We were
working in the same place, me in accounting, her up on the
second floor, in fabrics. That's how we met, in the Bougons'
family business. We took a good long look ahead, and what
we saw coming was an ulcer for me and a nasty menopause
for her. She wanted to travel and I liked to drive. Bougons-
Frères thought we were playing an April fool's joke on them,
because that was the day we handed in our resignations. Just
a twist of fate, letting us leave with a smile. They believed it
in the end, though. So did our office mates, the ones we saw
getting older every Christmas, telling stories about the good
old days that wheezed with asthmatic nostalgia.

We had some money in the bank, but mainly we had our
Saviem truck, and we spent our nest egg on a second van to

JOSEPH INCARDONA (1969–) lives and writes in Geneva.
His books include *Lonely Betty* (2010), *Remington* (2008),
Banana Spleen (2006), and *Le Cul entre deux chaises* (2001). This
story appears in his 2005 collection *Taxidermie*.

tow behind it. We adopted a nomadic life in an unusual way. The idea of selling French fries and merguez sausages, that was Odette's. We got our license without too much trouble: the mayor and the city hall clique thought Mami and Papi were a sweet old couple. We were treated to a full-page column in the local paper, with Odette and me looking blank in front of the sky-blue *À la bonne franquette* sign painted on the side of the Saviem. We headed south, to the sunshine. It wasn't new to us, but pretty sights are always nice when you haven't seen any for a long time.

Between rest stops and Sunday markets, the time flew by. Fries and sausages is what the sign said, but Odette actually whipped up fancier stuff, like paupiettes, or a tart she made with cumin, goat cheese, and spinach. Michelin-quality eats, made out of thin air. And she had a secret: she always cooked as if the world were going to end tomorrow. It gave a kind of urgency to the food, sort of spiced it up.

Time always passes too fast, and it had nearly passed us by, because we had kept on saying that we'd leave tomorrow. We hit the road just in time, avoiding rocking chairs by heading down winding roads instead of backing into the garage with our bifocals and old-age pensions.

So anyway, we're parked along one of those winding roads, waiting for a traveler with hunger pangs, and we see them swerve over to us. I could feel Odette get all giddy when they parked the motorcycle on its kickstand. The girl had blond hair and a cute little ass in her leather pants. The guy's beard made him look like a thug, but hey, he had wind in his hair and you've got to admire that, whatever they say.

They gave us nice, reassuring smiles, and scarfed down everything we had on the menu—four or five little pastries

Odette had fixed that morning. They sat at one of the plastic tables with Heineken umbrellas I'd set up not far away. The guy pulled out a bottle of booze, and we could hear them laughing as their Gauloises burned in the wind. When they came over to pay, I treated them to a shot of the hot coffee we kept in a thermos for special customers. The guy headed back to his bike. I saw the girl hesitate. There might have been regret in her eyes but I don't think she had any choice. She pulled out a gun.

"Hand over the cash, old man."

Odette and I watched each other turn pale. These things happened, and given a choice, I'd just as soon it be a twenty-year-old girl with blue eyes. I gave her everything in the drawer. Even the small change; you never know when it'll come in handy.

"Is that all?" she asked.

"Next time, come at the end of the day," I said, joking.

My voice was shaky, but I saw a dimple brighten her face. She pocketed the take and made tracks. But just as she was about to climb onto the Suzuki, she turned around and came trotting back to us, holding her helmet. Odette was in my arms, shaking with fear. It didn't even occur to me that this could be curtains for our little business. Her boyfriend yelled something at her from under his visor. The girl went up to Odette. She could have come to me, but one look at my face must tell you that I'm no kind of cook. What she had to say was strictly for Odette.

"Your pies are really good, Madame," she said breathlessly. "You'll have to give me the recipe, okay?"

Then she sprinted over to the bike and climbed on, and they shot off in a cloud of dust, gasoline, and burned rubber.

Translated by William Rodarmor

Even Me

Claire Julier

THEY'RE ALL HERE, even me. I couldn't miss a day like today. They're all there, hovering around her, and she's counting and re-counting them to make sure she isn't forgetting anyone. She checks one last time. Later she'll be able to say to her girlfriend, "There were forty-two of us. That's right, forty-two!" The friend won't know what to say. Serves her right. There were only twenty-three people at her house; the table was practically empty.

The men go off to watch television. There's a game on, I think. The women are there, around her. They talk about their bellies, bellies round with a child on the way, round after its arrival, still round because of the canapés they're

CLAIRE JULIER (1939–) is a cultural and literary critic and the author of several short story collections: *Entre-deux* (2007), *Les Désencontres* (2004), and *Couleur sépia* (2001). This piece is from her 1999 collection *La Pêcheuse d'eau*, which describes the often-tense relations between one family's generations. Note: A *calisson* is a lozenge-shaped candy made of iced marzipan. *Marrons glaceés* are candied chestnuts.

putting away. Me, I listen. I'm not allowed to say anything. "You're so thin, you look like a skinned cat. A bag of bones. And flat as a flounder, to boot. No ass, no hips. C'mon, eat a little something."

A plate is shoved under my nose. Round slices of bread smeared with dark paste with an anchovy on top. There are four left, surrounded by a bunch of lipstick-stained toothpicks. Bony anchovies and pointed things with red smears make me sick. I feel nauseated and I suddenly want to be outside, to feel the cold air on my body, to gulp it in. I search for the window. The smooth glass is hidden behind heavy, garnet-colored double curtains. You can't even see any light from outside. If I could tear away this mass of fabric, open the window, lean out, and twist my neck, maybe I'd be able to see a patch of sky beyond the walls opposite, the chimneys, and the television antennas. "What are you doing? You're completely crazy. That cold air's going to kill us. Eat, instead. A few extra pounds wouldn't do you any harm. Look at your sisters."

I look at them. They're all around her, along with her descendants and her great-descendants. The littlest ones, on their knees, sucking fingers dripping with spit. It's as sweet as a Jacques Brel song.

Forty-two! Yes, there were forty-two of us waiting around, with the women and children in the living room and the men next door in front of a giant screen. The meal will be served soon. We'll all get to sit in the special dining room with the white tablecloth, the fan-folded napkins, the whole kit and caboodle. The wine bottles will be laid in woven silver baskets for the occasion. Mistletoe is hanging from the chandelier, symbolic mistletoe placed right in the center of the table where it's impossible to pass by and kiss someone and wish them . . . what, exactly? Oh yes, a happy new year. Or no, that's next week. Today is just Christmas and we don't kiss. The Virgin gazes down, the donkey and the cow, hallelujah. all brothers and sisters. "Even you. Forty-two, I must have all forty-two! A day like today, you can make an effort." Her tone slows and drags; her voice quavers.

I'm there. An even number. I'm even me, eventually. I'm playing with words, shriveling up because I'm really not hungry and I can't eat any of the food being shoved under my nose. Stuffed turkey, something I've always hated. Its belly crammed with chestnuts and that heavy, sickly-sweet stuffing. I've hated it for as long as I can remember, and here it is sprawled on a plate, legs apart, skin spiky, stuffed to bursting with chestnuts.

Before that, there was cold, glassy-eyed fish, tarted up with parsley. "Go on, have some. You don't get fat from eating fish, and it makes you smart!" I don't answer. I'm squeezing my bread into a ball under the table. When it's packed good and tight, I might go do something with it. I don't know what yet.

Here come the desserts. Thirteen of them, because it's traditional. I'm choking on bites of these thirteen damned desserts. "There's so many of us, you have to learn to share, and on a day like today, you should think of the poor." I have half a date, a bit of *calisson,* and a big piece of *bûche de noël.* "There's a lot of *bûche* left, and I'm not about to throw it away. It cost a fortune." I doubt my ditching bits of dessert under the table will do the poor any harm.

Talk is flying by, over my head. Words clog my ears, but I'm not paying them any attention yet. I'm waiting. I have all the time in the world. It's sure to happen, sooner or later. The wrong word, a slap, tears, faces swollen with repressed rage. Maybe it'll happen when the presents are handed out next to the electro-neon-fluoro Christmas tree. Each person in a corner opening their presents, counting them, evaluating them. Tomorrow, she'll be able to tell her girlfriend, the one with only twenty-three guests, "I was so spoiled! I felt like a queen!" The friend will choke back her envy and say, "Well, of course, with so many children!"

On the floor, a kid is playing with the silvery ribbon. Another one attacks with a giant robot with flame-thrower eyes. On television, the Pope is firing off his message of peace. Someone turns up the volume. "You should all listen to him on a day like today. Even though you don't go to church, it'll do you good."

A tray with Champagne glasses passes under my nose. "You spilled your glass on purpose! Look at the floor! Think of how expensive Champagne is! You've always got to be the center of attention. If you were going to be so grumpy, I don't know why you bothered coming. We'd have been just fine with forty-one of us. Look at your sisters."

I look at them. They're sitting on the edge of their chairs with presents open on their laps. The one on the far end is pursing her lips, as if she's about to cry. Maybe things will get going over there. Her husband squeezes her shoulder, whispers a few words in her ear. She grips his hands, turns her face away. The storm has passed. It won't break. Too bad.

The children are blowing up the paper bags and popping them with their hands. The explosions drown out the midnight Mass that followed the pontifical message. A silver bowl with *marrons glacés* is passed from hand to hand. I half-swallow one, it catches in my throat, and the cold stares make me want to vomit even more. My head is spinning, and my sisters' faces seem to be merging into a single face that takes over the face of the queen sitting in the middle of the living room, enters her face, becoming one and the same mask. I'm not about to faint here, though, amid the smell of candied fruits and warm Champagne.

At last, a man starts to yell. A door slams. The whole room trembles. Behind the door, shouting. "Nothing's gonna stop me from leaving! I warned you!" "You can't leave, today of all days. It's Christmas. Think of the children!" "Papa, stay with us." "Maman, don't cry!"

"Aren't you ashamed of yourself in front of the children?" No, they're not ashamed. They yell even louder. The words rush out, choppy and confused, made still louder by the voices. No, they really aren't ashamed at all, not even of giving their tongues free rein, spilling the secrets of their sex.

"Come on, maman, don't cry!" "You! It's always the same thing when you're here. I just knew it. Your father must be turning in his grave. If he were still alive . . . !" I can see him rubbing his hands, precisely because he isn't here. No stuffed turkey, no dead-eyed flounder, no thirteen desserts while thinking of the poor. He's six feet under, all alone, in silence. He must love it.

Very slowly, I made my way to the Christmas tree, took my gift-wrapped present, and slipped out. I tossed the package onto the back seat. I knew that the pink ribbon and taped paper contained yet another grandmotherly white cotton nightgown with nice broderie anglaise or cross-stitching, picked up for a song from some market or a Chinese street vendor. "They're the only ones who still know how to do embroidery, but the fabric's no good. In France today unwed mothers don't want to work anymore; I don't know what they live on. Things are changing, and we may as well help out the Third World. Same thing with the supermarkets, full of fish from Africa."

I'll stick it in the closet, adding it to the pile. Guaranteed to yellow within the year. One of these days I'll tie them all together, and use them to either gag or hang myself.

Translated by William Rodarmor

Brasserie

Marie Rouanet

THE BRASSERIE where I went to eat looked like one of those English pubs that in turn looks like a living room or some wood-paneled German bakery. It had tables set apart in quiet corners, with lamps placed here and there like in a sitting room. There was a mezzanine, a creaky staircase of polished wood, and panes of beveled green glass revealing only the night aglow with the city's evening lights.

The walls kept the noise out, and the gentle warmth offered protection against the sharp winter cold.

MARIE ROUANET (1936–) is a French writer, ethnologist, and documentary filmmaker, as well as a composer and singer in Occitan. The author of many novels and essays, she is best known for her books *Luxueuse austérité* (2006) and *Nous les filles* (1990). "Brasserie" appears in Rouanet's 2002 short story collection *Enfantine*. It uses some words from south-central France's Aubrac region: a *buron* is a stone hut in the mountain pastures used for shelter and for cheese-making, under the supervision of the *buronnier*. *Roulles* are boys who work summers as cowherds.

I was hungry that evening, and had just ordered duck leg in honey sauce.

"What do you serve it with?" I asked the waitress.

"Fresh pasta."

"Spaghetti?"

"No, tagliatelli with butter."

"That'll be fine."

"Would you like something to drink?"

She brought me the wine list. I picked out the Lledoner pelut, a fairly rare Catalan Grenache.

"And a half-bottle of Lledoner."

I had brought a good book by an author I didn't know. I hadn't started it yet but I knew it was about a castrato.

Ever since I discovered countertenors and male sopranos, I had been fascinated by these voices.

Fascinated and disturbed by these rather androgynous creatures, I was sorry I could no longer hear them, sorry I could only imagine their singing from performers like Aris Christofellis. One particular version of Pergolesi's *Stabat Mater* has a duet between soprano and countertenor that showed the difference between the pure timbres of male and female voices, a piece that for me was simply angelic.

These were almost disembodied voices; listening to them reminded you of sounds that were not human: the mistral wind whistling through power lines, the wind mouthing a chimney pipe and singing through it, the note varying according to the degree of force, a long breath, so long it astonishes you, the way you are astonished when you listen to singers who seem never to breathe and to be possessed of endless air.

The book I was holding told the story of a year in the life

of a castrato and his initiation into adulthood, when as a passionate virgin he first knew love.

I was anticipating near-perfect pleasure, combining the delights of the palate, the body luxuriating in cozy comfort, and the mind relishing a special reading treat. A healthy appetite enhances the savor of food and a good book is good company.

I'd been seated beside the railing on the mezzanine floor, overlooking a few tables below.

This bird's-eye view gave me a kind of invisibility—who would think of looking upward? I started watching people eating and what they were eating, started listening too, setting aside the story of my delectable castrato.

A family was dining directly below me: a couple and a little girl. Only the child was facing me. I had a side view of the woman and could see only the man's back.

The little girl was very pale, with a faint bluish tinge to her skin, like some types of fine china. Dark hair grew very sparsely on the top of her head; she was almost bald. If I'd been sitting downstairs I wouldn't have noticed anything, but my view from above clearly revealed that on either side of her part a thin curtain of hairs—so few you could almost count them—wasn't enough to hide the whiteness of her skull.

I thought of several explanations: the girl had had cancer, the treatment had made her lose her hair. Then I reassured myself that her pale complexion or the effect of the light had fooled me, or that some children had very thin hair that would thicken with age.

The little girl did not speak; none of the trio said much, in fact. This corner of the restaurant was noticeably quiet.

The child, who must have been seven or eight years old, was very small, her chin barely reaching above the tabletop.

I started to read. I poured myself a little wine and began to sip it.

A voice pulled me out of the pleasant triangle—the wine, the story, and me—where I had settled.

"Come closer to the table."

It was the man who had spoken. He was talking to the girl. She didn't move.

"Come-clo-ser-to-the-ta-ble," he said again, in an astonishingly staccato voice.

The woman kept her eyes fixed on her plate. The girl looked at the man but still didn't move. Her eyes were huge, reminding me of crickets' eyes. They glittered, as dark as her hair, in her porcelain face. They were fringed with long straight lashes that lay on her cheeks.

"I told you to come closer," the man said, raising his voice.

At the same time he abruptly reached out a large hand and grabbed a fistful of the little girl's hair, pulling her head over her plateful of French fries.

A strangled noise came from the girl's throat and, although nothing else in her face changed, her mouth started to quiver. She was going to cry.

I couldn't see the man, just the back of his broad neck and his hands, so big that one of them could have covered that whole little face. His voice was raised again:

"And if you cry, I'll give you something to cry about."

The woman made a halfhearted gesture: "Oh, come on . . ."

"I like children who are well behaved," he said.

The man shook his hand, then used the other to pick off a hair twisted round his fingers.

Suddenly I understood the bald head. It owed nothing to illness or to nature.

Something icy touched my heart. My fine dinner and my good read were at an end.

The woman looked at the man and the child in turn. Perhaps sensing I was staring at the scene, she looked up toward the mezzanine. I could see in her eyes not only the urge to weep, but resignation as well. As if she were saying: that's just the way things are.

She murmured something to the man, probably telling him they were being watched. All I heard was his ringing reply:

"I don't give a shit."

The girl's face showed her struggle to fight back the tears. She succeeded. She was sitting very upright again, still staring straight at the man.

"Eat up," he said, perhaps so she would bow her head and stop looking at him.

My book was still open, but I had stopped reading. I wasn't interested in anything now except the pulled-out hair, the child's willpower, and the mother's attitude.

If that's her daughter, I thought, it's awful. How does she feel in the morning when she combs her hair?

What was ruining my evening must surely be ruining her life. What power stronger than this pain made her stay with this man? Every thought churning in my head was equally sinister.

The meal went on. The girl said nothing, the woman spoke so quietly that I couldn't hear anything. Only the man's words were understandable. He praised the meat. He praised the wine in a loud, clear voice.

Very slowly the girl finished her fries. Now she shrank

down in her chair. Before every movement, she looked up at the man. Before leaning back against the chair, before lifting first one hand, then the other, from the table and putting them on her knees.

"Sit up straight," the man ordered.

The woman intervened. She must have told him the girl wasn't hungry any more, that she had finished eating.

"If she's finished," he announced, "she won't get any dessert."

The girl didn't care. Her little hands stayed on her knees.

She looked around. Our eyes met. I smiled at her but she turned her head away, almost haughtily. There was no place for me in what she was living through.

Nothing, neither the excellent sauce—the perfectly cooked honey had colored it a rich brown—nor the magnificent glow of the Lledoner pelut could distract me from what I saw here and understood.

Left alone on her chair, the little girl seemed at peace.

And I started thinking about the young cowherds in the Aubrac *burons*, hired on for the summer grazing season. The boys were about twelve, and it was their job to round up straying cows; they were as quick as dogs and more intelligent. They did the dirty work, running through the cold night air to the far end of a field to bring back a forgotten tool. At meals, they were the last to be served and got the stalest bread.

In the evenings the adults would huddle round the fire. The best places were taken by the boss, the *buronnier*, then the workers, seated in order of importance and seniority, and finally the *roulles*, as the young cowherds were called. They might see the flames, but they didn't feel much of the heat.

On rainy evenings, the big, heavyset men would hang their wet clothes from the mantelpiece to dry, with the *roulles'* far from the fire. The next morning the boys would pull on their wet clothes and shoes again.

The men would say that the young ones needed to be toughened up, that they'd been through the same thing and it hadn't killed them. Sometimes one of the workers would be nastier than the others. He wouldn't stop at the usual ridicule and bullying. He would beat the boys, and rape them in the night.

Hatred would build over the summer seasons.

And sometimes, five or ten years later at a village festival, an aging former worker would find himself face to face with an unrecognizable young man. Yesterday's skinny little boy had hatched into an adult bursting with muscles and rage.

Under cover of night, he would wait for his former tormentor. He would throw him to the ground and attack him, kicking him in the back, the stomach, the belly, the groin. He would leave him lying there.

Some died as a result. Witnesses would say that the man had collapsed after drinking throughout the festival and frozen to death in the night. A terrible fall, a terrible night.

Doctors and police pretended to believe them.

But stories about the *roulles'* revenge are told on drunken evenings, when wine breaks down barriers and the desire for justice flares up from deep in people's minds, whole and hot as burning embers.

Translated by Jean Anderson

Spinach Should Be Cooked with Cream

Claude Pujade-Renaud

MIREILLE BOUGHT IT AT THE MARKET. She used to buy it frozen; it's quicker, but Antoine doesn't like it. She sorts the leaves one by one, then washes them thoroughly. As she blanches them, she watches them swell up, they look almost alive. Once they're out of the pot they shrink in a most alarming way. All those steps, just to wind up with this little heap of greenish glop! It fits between her palms. She squeezes it to get rid of the water. And still there's more. The pile gets even smaller. She keeps squeezing. It's making her hands ache. Especially after spending the day typing. She hears Antoine come in and hurries to dry her hands. They kiss. Antoine sets the kitchen table, sits down, and

CLAUDE PUJADE-RENAUD (1932–) has written more than twenty novels and short story and poetry collections. In 1994, she won the Prix Goncourt des lycéens for her novel *Belle mère*. She is also a dance teacher and has written a number of pedagogical texts relating to the body and the classroom. This piece is from her 1985 short story collection *Les Enfants des autres*.

starts on the cold cuts. Mireille nibbles at slices of salami, moving back and forth between the table and the stove. Antoine talks about organizational problems in his workshop. Mireille reheats the spinach. She adds some of the juices from last night's roast, then some croutons rubbed with garlic. Mireille is from Toulon, in the South, so she can't imagine cooking without garlic. She puts the dish of spinach on the table, sits down, and eats her slice of ham. Antoine serves himself, takes a bite, and says,

"Spinach should be cooked with cream."

He keeps on eating, showing no signs of disliking it. His pronouncement wasn't aggressive. But it was final, Mireille thinks. Antoine has definite opinions. About politics, sports, and food. He announces them calmly. Sometimes Mireille wonders where and how he picked them up. On Antoine's lips they seem as natural as the color of his eyes. They're perfectly ordinary. Or are they? Mireille picks listlessly at her spinach, even though the garlic makes it very tasty. They watch a movie on TV, talk about it as they get undressed, and make love with gusto. Before she falls asleep Mireille is troubled by a recurring question: where did he get the idea spinach should be cooked with cream?

Next morning at the office, the question takes a different shape: who gave him that idea? Mireille is typing a report. Probably Nicole, his first wife. They were divorced over ten years ago. Nicole went off to Africa with her second husband. Mireille and Antoine met after that. She puts in a fresh sheet of carbon paper. She realizes she's hardly thought about Nicole until now. She has a sudden vision of her, looking creamy and appetizing. Without breaking her rhythm, Mireille asks Gisèle at the next desk:

"Do you know how to cook spinach with cream?"

"Yes, in a soufflé. I'll write down the recipe for you, if you like."

A little too late, Mireille realizes making a soufflé takes more time than she'd planned for. After you cook the spinach, you have to completely drain and mince it. She really should buy a food processor. Let the béchamel sauce thicken, beat in the egg yolks and the cream, grate the Gruyère and a little nutmeg, stir it into the sauce, beat the whites—her wrist is still sore—fold it in lightly, butter the soufflé dish. She puts it in the oven. Antoine comes in.

"Isn't it ready yet?"

He reads *France-Soir*, propping his elbows on the Formica table. Mireille keeps an eye on the soufflé as it rises. Even though he shows no sign of impatience, Antoine's waiting annoys her. Usually Mireille organizes things so dinner is cooked when he gets home. He has to commute a lot farther than she does. Before Antoine, she paid no attention to mealtimes. She ate when she was hungry. Or didn't eat. Did Nicole . . . ? The soufflé puffs up. Mireille enjoys watching this gradual metamorphosis. It starts to brown on top. Should she cover it with a piece of baking paper? Gisèle didn't say anything about that. Mireille washes the dishes. Whenever she fixes something a little fancy there are pots and pans everywhere. Was Nicole a tidy cook, was dinner always ready on time? Looking at Antoine, Mireille gets irritated. He must have read his newspaper like this, completely absorbed, while Nicole bustled about. Just by sitting at a table and waiting, he'd managed to impose another woman's movements on Mireille. Without her noticing. Probably without his noticing, either. It happened without their realizing. He had carried on in his usual fashion, just as peacefully as he read his *France-Soir*. With all the violence of his good-natured rigidity. His usual fashion, or theirs? That's the way things are: they go to the mountains for their vacation, to the early show at the movies on Saturday evening, Chasselas is better than Muscatel, they listen to RTL radio, spinach should be cooked with cream. Mireille opens the oven. The soufflé looks wonderful. It collapses as soon as she puts a spoon into it.

So does Mireille.

"It's not bad, but you should find a recipe for spinach with cream."

"But there *is* cream in it!"

"Really? You can't tell."

Can he only tell with an exact copy? Next day, when Gisèle asks how the soufflé went, Mireille doesn't know what to say. She ate it on autopilot. Antoine needs the taste of before. Mireille has to give this back to him. Eventually she finds the proper recipe in a book she borrows from the social club library at work. Antoine seems content. He doesn't make any more comments, he just swallows. The spinach must have gone down to join the previous lot. Life imitates life. Mireille stands frozen beside the table. Antoine looks at her.

"Aren't you eating anything?"

"Yes, of course."

She sits down. She chews conscientiously. Exhausted, as if a green diarrhea, a slimy spinach pulp, were pouring endlessly from her body. A sieve. The past passes through her. A woman in a kitchen serving Antoine spinach cooked with cream, for all eternity. That's the way it is. Carrying on. Anyone can replace anyone else. All it takes is the right amount of cream. Both at the table and in bed? Mireille tries to avoid that slippery slope. Nicole wasn't just anyone. Mireille is, though. Bland, like her own cooking. Garlic and basil don't make up for anything. And besides, she can hear it now: "Nicole Izanic" sounds right, rolls off the tongue. Whereas "Mireille Izanic" is awkward, it's lumpy. She thought she and Antoine were so close. This whole cream thing is much more serious than a matter of culinary differences between Brittany and Provence. Somewhere, here but not here, there's a white-tiled kitchen. Mireille can see copper pots, a wooden spice rack, a potted hydrangea. A woman moving back and forth. Mireille gets up and serves the cheese.

For Mireille the day of the soufflé was the beginning of her depression. Or her dispossession. She has practically no appetite, has more and more trouble sleeping. A strange dream keeps recurring. A blurry shape in a flowing robe is walking ahead of her. Mireille has to step exactly in its footprints. She would like to see the blurry shape's face. But each time it turns around, Mireille wakes up. Or her possession. Sometimes sentences descend upon her:

"Food is devouring me."

Fixing meals becomes both disgusting and an obsession. Strangely, Mireille spends more time on it than necessary. And even more time thinking about it. Planning a simple meal, what she'll need to buy, the various steps, it all preoccupies and overwhelms her. While typing at the office, she obsesses over it:

"Do I have enough butter left for the pasta?"

"I'll have to keep the sauce hot in the double boiler while we eat the cucumbers."

"I'll have to remember to preheat the oven for the vegetables."

Food gnaws away at her as she slowly loses her appetite. Her obsession spreads like a greasy stain over the rest of her everyday married life. Antoine's slightest gestures, his most innocent comments, are now suspect. Whether they are his own or not is no longer certain. And those mouths everywhere, all those open mouths demanding to be fed at fixed times. The washing machine, a great gleaming mouth. Fill it, empty it. Like the body. What comes out of the body smells bad. The machine excretes cleanliness. Other than that, Mireille can't see any difference anymore. Sucking, stubborn mouths. Always greedy for more. Antoine's mouth. The sink's, gurgling away. The vacuum cleaner's. It snores. Antoine does, too; now that she's not sleeping well she notices this. The toilet's. The staring eyes Mireille used to see in its depths when she was a child are back. Cannibal eyes. The old terrors under the surface. Under her skin, a woman called Nicole. From time to time, when she's alone, Mireille tries to pull herself together. She talks to herself out loud:

"Am I going nuts or what?"

Maybe she should go see a doctor? She doesn't dare, it's not an illness you can talk about. Or cure with drugs probably. Mireille hates herself for being so naïve. She was settled comfortably in the illusion of an easygoing present, and is amazed that spinach with cream was enough to open up such a crack. But maybe it was there already? The crack radiates out into previously unknown territory. Mireille starts to have nightmares, sticky, sweating anxiety attacks, feels disoriented and exhausted the moment she wakes up. As if she were occupying a place designated in advance by established and inscrutable habits. Or as if she no longer had a place to be.

In the café after lunch in the canteen, her friends from work are concerned.

"You've lost weight," says Simone. "You're in a bad way."

"And you're eating less and less," notes Maryse.

"Yes, and your typing is a lot slower," Gisèle adds. "What's the matter?"

"I'm fed up with cooking."

"Me too!"

"So am I!"

Mireille doesn't know how to explain it to them. It's so uninteresting, but at the same time this is what's happening to her.

"Food is killing me. When I get home I just want to go to bed, I feel like sleeping all day, ignoring the alarm clock, I want to forget . . . "

"You're depressed," Simone announces. "You need to see a shrink."

"A what?"

"A psychologist. It's obvious cooking isn't the only source of your problems."

Maryse interrupts, sharply: "Well, I for one don't believe in your middle-class psychotherapy! It all comes down to the way society's organized. If there was more equality between men and women in the workplace, there'd be a bit more equality at home."

Mireille doesn't think so.

Neither does Gisèle, who says, "You're like the rest of us, you've had enough of fixing meals every day. That's all there is to it. It comes and goes, you just get on with it."

Simone doesn't agree.

"If she really can't stand to feed Antoine this way, it's because it's all over between them. You have to have the courage to face facts."

Mireille doesn't dare tell them she loves Antoine. She believes he loves her too. She doesn't say anything. Gisèle offers her another cup of coffee.

"It'll do you good."

A few days later, Maryse, the union representative, bumps into Mireille in the locker room.

"Haven't you ever been a union member?"

"Er, yeah, but a long time ago."

"Don't you want to sign up again?"

Mireille hesitates. She's had other things on her mind, she's a bit out of touch.

Maryse doesn't insist. "It's your decision."

"Well, I will, then. How much are the membership dues now?"

That evening, Antoine voices his opposition. He has always refused to join the union.

"The unions are just as corrupt as the bosses," he says.

The statement echoes in Mireille's ears the same way the one about spinach did. That same calm certainty. She doesn't have it herself. Did Nicole? Mireille doesn't go to union meetings but she keeps her card.

Ever since the business with the union, Antoine has gotten more and more interested in his soccer club. Not content with playing on Sundays, he decides to train the junior team two evenings a week. Afterward, he has a meal with them in a little restaurant near the stadium. Mireille breathes a bit easier. She gets back some of her enjoyment of food. Sitting on the floor in a corner of the bedroom, nibbling at something. Or in the bathroom, snuggled against some cushions between the bidet and the bathtub. Picking at leftovers as she listens to the transistor radio. A chunk of cheese, a handful of lettuce leaves without even any dressing, an apple to crunch without peeling it. In no particular order. Not sitting at the table any more, not planning anything, breaking the routine. Mireille drinks straight from the bottle, she wipes her mouth with the back of her hand. She lets time pass between bites, she closes her eyes as she chews, she relaxes. The flavors return. Slowly, the weariness fades away.

Her friends at work are quietly supportive. Gisèle helps out when she misses her deadlines. Simone keeps magazines and books for her. Mireille remembers that she used to like browsing in bookstores. On Sundays when Antoine is away on a soccer trip, Maryse invites Mireille over. Maryse is single, she doesn't cook. On a coffee table she sets out cold cuts, fresh fruit, and a fruit tart from the bakery. She plays records and avoids making political speeches. She fills Mireille's glass, makes her a nice cup of coffee. It feels good to be given food and drink by someone else, even in a rudimentary way. Months pass. The exhaustion passes. Mireille gains back a little weight. She's sleeping better. She notices that the dream about the blurry shape has gone.

One after the other, the mouths close. Antoine's mouth becomes affectionate again. At the table with him, Mireille has a little more appetite. For her birthday he gives her a slow cooker. Mireille can go off to work, leaving a nice little ragout to simmer. The slow cooker does the thinking for her and turns off all by itself. Simone tries to explain to her that household appliances make women even more alienated. Obviously, because Mireille now gets up even earlier to start her lamb stew before rushing off to work. Mireille smiles and lets her talk. Anyway, fixing meals doesn't bother her so much anymore. She even tries a few experiments, again following Gisèle's advice. Antoine accepts them without hesitation. Just the same, Mireille still makes spinach with cream. Every time she does, she checks the recipe, copied into a notebook. You have to work at love.

It's five years later. Antoine is eating his spinach in silence. Mireille makes it on autopilot these days. It's part of her life now. Antoine cleans his plate carefully and helps himself to some salad.

"You know, the way you fix spinach is a bit bland. The cream makes it even mushier. Couldn't you find a different recipe?"

Mireille looks at him without speaking. That evening, in bed, she admits to herself that love can be insipid sometimes. Antoine wraps himself in sleep. She broods. What if she was the one who turned the spinach into a ghost? Nicole never came back from Africa. Might it have been only Mireille's mind she haunted? But what about Antoine's quiet insistence? That last sentence of his has come a bit late. He probably needed some time too. As Mireille did, to get over her all-devouring depression. All by herself, supported by the kindness of her friends.

Mireille remembers: even at school she had problems with verbs. To do, to be. Or not to be. The past isn't simple.

Life is complicated. It's easy to put garlic back into the spinach. But what do you put back into love? Mireille turns onto her side to go to sleep. She misses her lost dream about the blurry shape. She'd be strong enough now to look it in the face.

Translated by Jean Anderson

The Legend of Bread

Michel Tournier

ONCE UPON A TIME, in the farthest reaches of France, where the land ends and the ocean begins—in the Finistère region of Brittany, to be precise—there were two small villages forever pitted against each other in rivalry. One of them was called Plouhinec, the other, Pouldreuzic. The villagers never missed a chance to clash. The people of Plouhinec, for example, played the *biniou* bagpipes better than anyone else in Brittany. Which was reason enough for Pouldreuzic to completely ignore that instrument and make a great show of preferring the bombard, a kind of flageolet related to the

---

MICHEL TOURNIER (1924–) is a French writer and journalist who has won such awards as the Grand Prix du roman de l'Académie française in 1967 for *Vendredi ou les limbes du Pacifique* (1967), a retelling of the Robinson Crusoe story, and the Prix Goncourt for *Le Roi des aulnes* (1970, tr. *The Ogre*). His books often deal with myth and fantasy and are inspired by traditional German culture, Catholicism, and the philosophy of Gaston Bachelard. This story is from his 1989 collection *Le Médianoche amoureux.*

---

oboe and the clarinet. And so it went, in every possible way. If one group grew artichokes, the other grew potatoes; some force-fed their geese, the others fattened pigs; the women from one village wore simple, chimney-like headdresses, in the other village they worked theirs into little lace skyscrapers. The rivalry even included apple cider, Plouhinec shunning it because Pouldreuzic was famous for it. So what did they drink in Plouhinec, you may wonder. They drank something made not from apples but from pears, and for that reason called perry.

Needless to say, they didn't eat the same kind of bread in Plouhinec and Pouldreuzic. Plouhinec's specialty was a hard, crusty bread that sailors stocked up on before they set off to sea, because it would keep indefinitely. Instead of this Plouhinec hardtack, the bakers in Pouldreuzic made a soft bread that melted in your mouth and was best eaten hot from the oven, called brioche.

Things got complicated the day the Pouldreuzic baker's son fell in love with the Plouhinec baker's daughter. Their dismayed families did their best to talk the two youngsters out of such an unnatural union, which faced every kind of difficulty, but in vain: Gaël wanted Guénaële, and Guénaële wanted Gaël.

Fortunately, Plouhinec and Pouldreuzic are not close neighbors. Look at the map of Finistère and you will see a village halfway between the two: Plozevert. Since Plozevert didn't have a bakery at the time, Gaël's and Guénaële's parents decided to set their children up there. They would be married in Plozevert, too; that way, neither Pouldreuzic nor Plouhinec would be shamed. At the wedding banquet, they would eat artichokes and potatoes, goose and pork, and wash it all down with cider and perry.

But which bread to put on the table? That problem wasn't quite so easy to solve. The parents' first thought was to serve equal amounts of hard bread and brioches. But the children objected: it was a wedding, after all, and what's more, a wedding of two bakers. So they would have to find a way to marry the hard bread and the brioche, as well. In short, the new bakery was under an obligation to create a new kind of bread, Plozevert bread, as closely related to Plouhinec's crusty bread as it was to Pouldreuzic's soft bread. But how could they do this? How could they make bread that was both crusty and soft?

Two solutions seemed possible. Gaël suggested to Guénaële that they model their creation on crabs and lobsters. The hard part of these creatures is on the outside, the soft part inside. But Guénaële countered with the example of rabbits, cats, fish, and children. There the soft part—the flesh—is on the outside, the hard part—the bones—on the inside. She even remembered the two scientific words that describe this difference: lobsters are *crustaceans*, rabbits are *vertebrates*.

So the choice was between two sorts of hard-soft bread: crustacean bread, with a crust forming a kind of shell around the soft part, and vertebrate bread, with the crust hidden away inside the thick, soft part.

They set to work, each following his or her own inspiration. It was immediately obvious that crustacean bread is a lot easier to bake than vertebrate bread. When a ball of dough is put in the oven, its surface dries, browns, and hardens while the dough stays white and soft on the inside. But how can you make vertebrate bread? How can you get a hard crust on the inside of the loaf?

Gaël triumphed with his crustacean bread, but felt pained by his fiancée's failures. It wasn't as though the little baker Guénaële lacked resourcefulness! She knew that the heat of the oven created the crust. So the vertebrate bread needed to be cooked not from the outside, as happens in an oven, but from the inside. That's why she had the idea of thrusting a red-hot iron rod into the dough, like a kind of poker. You should have seen her wielding that poker like a smoking-hot weapon! She gritted her teeth, stuck out her chin, and impaled the loaves on her fiery sword. Watching her, Gaël felt a chill run down his spine. What in his fiancée's heart and mind could inspire this strange combat and the ardor with which she threw herself into it, he wondered. What if it wasn't always loaves of bread she skewered with her glowing poker?

But what did it matter, anyway? Guénaële wasn't getting anywhere, and by the time the wedding day arrived only the crustacean bread had been perfected. In fact, it was on that very day that the bread we now know so well—the baguette, with its golden crust and velvety soft interior—was first officially tasted.

Does that mean the vertebrate bread was completely forgotten? Not at all. Over the years that followed it would win a stunning victory, full of tenderness and poetry. Gaël and Guénaële had a little boy whom they named Anicet—like anise—in the hope this fragrant name would help him to make a place for himself in their business. And they weren't disappointed, because it was he who, at the age of five, gave his mother the idea that would lead to vertebrate bread. All he did was to eat brioche and a piece of chocolate for his afternoon snack. Watching him with his brioche in one hand and his piece of chocolate in the other, his mother suddenly slapped her forehead and rushed into the bakery. She had just realized that a bar of chocolate would provide the bone, the spine, the hard part of the bread.

That very evening, the first little *pains au chocolat* in history went on display in the window of the Plozevert bakery. They would soon conquer the world and bring pleasure to children everywhere.

Translated by Jean Anderson

Oysters

Fabrice Pataut

OUR HOUSE IS A VERY ANCIENT ONE. Our genea-
logical tree goes back to the twelfth century and includes
the most illustrious members of the great families in the
huge beds that stretched along the coast of Europe from
Denmark to Portugal. According to my mother, legend has
it that one of our first cousins, using just a grain of sand and
a great deal of sodium carbonate, gave the world the famous
Peregrine, which Phillip II bought in 1579. That pear-shaped
pearl weighed 34 carats and was the size of a pigeon egg.

FABRICE PATAUT (1957–)is a French writer whose books
include *En haut des marches* (2007), *Tennis, socquettes et abandon*
(2003), and *Aloysius* (2001). This story is from his 2005 collection *Trouvé dans une poche*, which won the Prix de la Nouvelle
from the Académie française.

Note: The "ferdydurkist" at the end of the story would be a
fan of the 1937 novel *Ferdydurke* by the Polish writer Witold
Gombrowicz. Considered a masterpiece of European modern-
ism, its style parodies common literary forms in prewar Polish
literature.

My sisters and I belong only to the poor branch, which hails from Marennes. That's where our mother was born, as were all our female ancestors on our mother's side, in fact. Papa, a magnificent five-inch Belon oyster with the promise of a brilliant, adventuresome future, piteously ended his days in a salt marsh at the mouth of the Seudre River. As fate would have it, an early-rising and fairly tipsy oysterman bumped Papa's shell with the edge of his rubber boot, sending him flying onto a pile of detritus, before the horrified eyes of his despairing and helpless mate.

From there he was picked up by the local garbage collectors, big husky guys who casually tossed him into a huge gray plastic bag. The bag promptly split, spilling some of its contents into a gutter, and a pernicious stream of water sent Papa straight into the sewers. He gave up the ghost in the bowels of subterranean northern Venice before sinking somewhere off the coast. The story was repeated to us—with the usual distortions—by girlfriends who lived in the bed next to the river's mouth.

So we grew up as orphans and somewhat dishonored by this tragedy. Then we were orphaned again when we were scooped up and put in large metal cages, because Maman disappeared during the operation. More than anyone, she'd had a deep nostalgia for our ancient, wild life. Because there was a time when our ancestors, left to their own devices, could freely travel wherever they wanted, and even go as far as chilly Albaek Bay on vacation.

As culinary objects, we live a life that would bore even the most serious of men to tears. That poor life consists in simply letting ourselves fatten in so-called *claire* beds. Some of us settled there. That's where my two sisters found their respective husbands, a pair of dullards who had shared a rack when they were young spats. Now left entirely alone, I placidly gained a good dozen grams. Needless to say, dear reader, the others all began to hate the nice fat one in less time than it takes to tell. That was to be expected. I was my mother's true daughter and was dying to travel on my own, to find the one who would swallow me properly. I certainly didn't want to hang around on some miserable rack waiting for Oyster Charming to show up.

"Crazy," "eccentric," "a witch," some even called me. In Marennes, where tongues wagged overtime to make my life miserable, I will always be the *Huître Galeuse*—the Bad Oyster—a title that does me the greatest honor and will raise me far above the provincial belfries for centuries to come.

The gossip spread quickly. I sensed that Maman was lost forever. What was the point of being stuck here? I decided to leave my so-called family once and for all. In His generous wisdom, God gave us our very useful shell, that little house on our back that makes it so easy to move around. In a beautiful, metaphorical gesture, I tossed Phillip II and his pearl to the dungeons along with my ancestors and all that withered, outdated past. Without remorse, I decided to live beyond the protective shade of the family tree.

Come nightfall, I slipped into the neighboring bed. I had been told that you ate better there. In fact, you simply ate more, but that suited me perfectly. More than anything, I had to become fat, as pleasingly plump as Andrea Ferreol, an actress for whom I have nothing but the greatest admiration. I wanted to become enormous and ready to eat, and do it in record time. I stuffed myself every day. I ate like a real pig. I can't even count the bellyfuls of lichen and seaweed I washed down with sea breeze and salt water. One day I even found myself eyeing a little *fine de claire*, ready to take a bite of her.

By the time I set off for La Tremblade, where new beds awaited us, I had already gained a gram. At Port-des-Barques, three more. Six at Arcachon. I was at the peak of that contagious euphoria that always precedes great departures and big decisions. My blue-green mantle—the sign of our Marennes origin—had finally reached the proper size. I never felt more desirable.

If you're a worldly type, Arcachon represents a decisive stage. From there, you leave for Paris. Everything that has gone before is just an initiation, a slow evolution of the self, a boring seminar where you spend your time dreaming of grand boulevards, of fine dining on terraces, of strings of pearls around the necks of those legendary Parisian women, and especially, of moustaches. The *nec plus ultra*, they say.

Jacqueline, one of my few girlfriends in Port-des-Barques, had told me that she had it on good authority that in Paris (and only there, of course), a man might without warning:

(a) choose you from a tray with the look of a connoisseur
(b) squirt lemon juice on you
(c) swallow you whole, raw, and
(d) drink your liquor, taking care to add, "They're delicious."

The use of the plural is a bit vexing, of course, since it represents a peremptory negation of our distinctive oysterish individuality. (Or is it "oysterlike"? This endless waiting is getting me all mixed up.) Anyway, as you see—and this is what I was getting at—it is a negation of our distinctive individuality as oysters, the expression of a haughty and almost certainly Parisian arrogance that paradoxically lowers us to the level of generic entities of no special flavor.

But in spite of all that, I wanted to know. What could it be like to feel those famous human whiskers brush your damp mantle as you then slide down the practiced esophagus of a businessman or a fashionable—considering what we cost—writer? But above all, the peak experience must be that brief moment when you remain in your gourmet's mouth, floating between the tongue and the palate of the man who chose you, tossed between dentition and taste buds, as you cast one last look at the inside of his lips, even before your other half has been set on the crushed ice next to the other empty shells.

I meditated a long time on the terrifying dexterity that great men must have, and was quite determined not to wind up like an idiot in the mouth of some beardless boy, no matter how handsome. Leaving this world without ever knowing the tickle of whiskers on the edge of my mantle would amount to an unforgivable mistake. Not only a mistake of taste, but something much more serious: something that would rob my life of its meaning at the very last minute.

Crammed in with other anonymous oysters in undignified propinquity, I was very ill at ease in the large wooden crate taking us to Austerlitz station. Numbered and feeling tired, I slept badly. The length of the trip, which after all was merely the penultimate obstacle to overcome before real life, was just a series of little fugues and variations on a unique theme.

The hand. A hand. The choice is yours, I don't care. I need one, with or without a ring. Brown or blond hairs suggest that the mustache will also be . . . A nervous hand. A soft hand . . . The veins . . . The nails always well trimmed. Too small, almost feminine. Or, to the contrary, strong and muscled, the wrist bone standing out from the flesh of the palm. Approaching the tray with determination. No . . . Not quite . . . Or not yet . . . Hesitating. Now he turns around to gently touch his female tablemate. "You go ahead, darling, please." *Ah zut!* Not that! Not a woman . . . And I almost forgot: the forks—*oyster* forks, they're called. Those tiny little forks that free us from our shells so smoothly. To have a deadly trident right at hand is a privilege we share with our cousins the snails—and periwinkles, of course; I almost forgot. Finally, the moustaches, lined up around the table: straight, brush, waxed, curled, even imperial (though very out of favor since the 1870 siege).

I was finally about to doze off when they unloaded us from the train. As yet unknown sounds were to be heard: whistles, hurried steps, clicking heels and clattering carts. Sharp knocks. My liquor going *splish-splash* against my shell. Thwack! We were stacked on top of other wooden crates. And all of this in total darkness, if you please. Pitch black. I was again about to nod off when I felt our crate being powerfully lifted into the air and it was then that we began to clearly hear something (I learned what it was later that evening): the distinctive rumble of the streets of Paris.

The distant sound of horns, the nearby squeaking of leather soles on dusty pavement, the scratch of the match lighting the cigarette of a pedestrian stopped at a red light. All these sounds were as if multiplied, rearranged in some

gigantic shuffling machine that was itself replicated to infin-
ity, plunging into the equally infinite labyrinth of avenues,
streets, alleys, cul-de-sacs, water courses, schoolyards, and
market squares, joining the tumult of neighborhoods near
and far with the din from distant suburbs, all of whose combined echo formed an acoustic bell over the capital. From the
depths of our crate we could clearly and distinctly perceive
this truly characteristic Latin and barbarian cacophony. *Non
tantem latina suava sed etiam barbara crudelis cacophonians.*

So I had arrived. We must've already been beyond the
station precinct. Our crate, stamped "Arcachon," hung
briefly in the air, swung quickly to the left, then jerked to
a stop. I bumped against my neighbor and promptly apolo-
gized. Then there was another bang to the right. "That one
goes to Fouquet's." And blam! We were lowered one floor
and landed on a hard surface. Doors opened and closed, and
we started our first and final journey in a traffic jam. Feeling
somewhat anxious because of all these new sounds, I took it
on myself to inquire of our destination from my neighbor,
trying my best not to seem too naïve.

"To Fouquet's, my dear," she said. "To Fouquet's, of
course. Haven't you heard? I already knew. What do you
think? It's probably written on the crate," she added sharply.
"First, because we are true oysters, not Portuguese. Second,
we are *fines de claire.* Third, we are number 4's—the very
best." (To her mind that figure was probably the equivalent
of a number of medals or noble titles.) "Finally, you must
never forget that we are from Port-des-Barques," she concluded haughtily.

What a snob! Why in the world couldn't those poor
Portuguese get into the same restaurants? I wondered. My

cosmopolitan mother had never mentioned this remarkable fact. To hold up my end of the conversation, I made a very general comment about the nature of a certain part of man's pilose system, and how it is displayed to especially fine effect around a good table. This deeply displeased her. For her, good taste absolutely rejected pilosity.

"They say that the Champs is very different these days," she said, quickly changing the subject. "Full of tourists in shorts. Don't you find that simply *in-cre-di-ble*? Personally, I think something should be done about it! On the Champs Elysées! My great-grandmother, who like every member of the family gloriously ended her days at Fouquet's, was swallowed there by Offenbach in 1864. Quite a memorial, you must admit! You know, there are times in life when one must set aside one's petty prejudices. Just think, he was humming a tune from *La Belle Hélène* three months before its premiere at the Théâtre des Variétés and tapping out the rhythm on her shell. What inspiration! What brilliance! Some people tell me, "It's the smell of the sea," and I reply, "It's family." We have a particular gift for feeding the inspiration of geniuses. Even small geniuses." (She wore a look of helpless pique as she said that.) "But I have not given up hope of restoring the family name."

"I'm sure you will," I said encouragingly.

"Listen, I'm going to take a little nap," she said. "I want to look fresh for tonight. Best of luck, in case I don't meet you on the tray."

The blast of chill air across the back of my shell woke me around midnight. At first I couldn't see in the dim light of the ground-floor room. The bay windows were partly open and I noticed that the acoustical bell over the capital had changed. The click of heels now had a relaxed tempo. A delicious cool feeling reminded me that I had just been prepared. I had missed that episode while I was asleep. Our collective memory is full of glimpses of flashing knives, as common as those wielded by denizens of bars where you dance the tango until dawn. Even without ever experiencing it, we all know that your shell will creak and that the raw, dry light of a brasserie chandelier will someday blind you. Maybe that's as far as you'll get. It happened to my uncle from Buenos Aires, who was passed up by Borges when he was eating with his mother. ("Jorgito, you aren't going to leave the last one, are you?" asked Doña Leonora. "*Creo que si*," replied her illustrious son, who suddenly found himself thinking of a lively tune from *West Side Story*.)

Hmm, the snob from Port-de-Barques wasn't on my tray, I noticed. Was she at the next table, where people were speaking German, and talking about Napoleon's tomb? I hoped with all my heart that it had ended long ago for her, thanks to the appetite of a plump, satisfied-looking gentleman.

But enough diversions! What did the other tables matter? My full attention turned to . . . him. I had spotted him and his handlebar moustache right away. His left hand was regularly sneaking under the tablecloth toward the woman next to him. Did I really have such poor taste, as my old rack-mates in Marennes used to suggest? But I ask you: how could one resist this dark-haired, handsomely handled man? Nothing, I say, nothing in his general appearance could prevent him from putting a hand wherever it seemed fitting, while extending the other to the tray in the center of the table. Not to underestimate the woman sitting next to him, however. Her power was clearly considerable. The bitch might yet manage to ruin my last evening.

What in the world could she be telling him that was so interesting?

"That's all terribly fascinating," she drawled, looking a bit dazed. (Handlebar was telling her—you'll never guess— about shellfish.) "But you see, I actually despise them. I never, ever, eat oysters or crustaceans. Of course, I share your astonishment. It's very rare. Even when my late husband was the British ambassador to . . . to . . . That's funny, I've completely forgotten where we were. Well anyway, we lived there for ten years. And in all those ten years near the sea, I swear I never touched a single one of those things. And yet, in their language, all twelve months of the year have an 'r' in them," she added, wrinkling her nose to under-score her witticism.

At that, she raised her chin to receive general approba-tion, and elegantly attacked her toast with foie gras, while the hand of the dashing young man with the manicured nails and handlebar mustache consoled her underneath her napkin. Later that night, with her lips pressed against his earlobe, she would murmur to him the marvelous names of those ocher, syrupy months: *Ravounistar, Ravounibour, Ravounisman*, and many other things as well.

At this point, his fingernail lay on the edge of my shell, though for strictly demonstrative purpose. I used the occa-sion to puff up my Marennes mantle. Did he feel a slight pressure on his fingertip? For the first time in my short life as an oyster, an irresistible desire raced through my inverte-brate body: to be taken immediately, without preliminaries, *rapidus velox*, and without lemon. Then and there. To feel the special oyster fork perform its age-old task, releasing me from my shell, to feel the young man's lips greedily suck me in, sending me flowing deep down his throat, etc. To remain forever in that gastric tomb, still whole and barely chewed. Today? Tomorrow?

But Handlebar wasn't paying me the slightest attention, the ungrateful wretch. He was much too busy hustling this old, slightly dotty ambassador's wife who, thank God, thought me unsuitable to eat. Then, like a brave little tailor, he started attacking the court-bouillon langoustines while turning the part of his body unconnected to his left hand to the other side of the table. There, I was distressed to realize, my life as a young oyster could well end in indignity. People were eagerly discussing literature, and a young blonde was reproaching an older man of using too many simpering expressions in his latest novel.

"That girl's right, you know," the old ambassador's wife whispered into handsome Handlebar's ear. "I've read him, and all that twee stuff is a crashing bore."

As for me, I had the sinking feeling that I had fallen on the wrong side of life. The real drama was being played out over there. I'd been waiting half an hour without accomplishing my goal. I was sure that Handlebar was big and strong, like Papa's garbage collectors. It was a terrible waste to have dragged myself all the way from La Tremblade when the evening's outcome wasn't looking very promising. I was now alone in the center of the tray. The ice was starting to melt, and the waiter would soon come by to get me.

At the end of the table, people were fussing around an older man. Handlebar, who was one of those clever lads who know when the wind is shifting, stupidly scraped his chair to warn the assembly that he also planned to participate, and that his contribution was worth waiting for. Twisting himself this way and that, he planted both elbows on the table as a sign of attention. He started to take an interest in the blonde, who just a moment ago had thought that there were too many expressions of a certain kind in a certain novel.

Our twee writer had set his sights on her. She was now visibly weakening. "Well, all right, let's just say on each page." Soon it will be each line again. I know them. Admitting defeat—didn't I tell you?—she confessed herself ready to read the next manuscript right away. Oh, really? It's done? At your place? Hot off the press? All finished? Ready for me? That's fantastic! This very evening? You can rummage in your desk drawer and I will stand behind you waiting, hands behind my back. After dinner of course I'd love to thank you because in the end, she rather liked all this cul-cul slaveringky. Maybe a pilgrimage to the home country, oh yes. I too want plains, low mountains with dark greenery, and cold, blue cities.

"To Warsaw with you," she cried, toasting him enthusiastically.

"It's a deal. *Ah là là!* You French! I very much like your language—husky and velvety," he purred to the very newest ferdydurkist. "And in the meantime, *cariñita*, I'll fix the last one for you."

Translated by William Rodarmor

Eating

Cyrille Fleischman

IN SPITE OF THE ORGANIZERS' PROMISES, no one was buying the works that he sat ready to sign.

People just went home after the reading, saying, "I have to get up early tomorrow," or "My brother already has your book; he'll lend it to me," or something along those lines.

Preverman remained alone behind the trestle table on which the association's secretary had set a stack of copies of the Yiddish poetry magazine he edited.

He never sold anything, except that one time when someone came up and asked to buy a magazine. He was so sur-

---

CYRILLE FLEISCHMAN (1941–2010) was a lawyer and writer whose tales were mostly set in the old Jewish Marais neighborhood of Paris. In addition to his popular *Métro Saint-Paul* trilogy, his books include *Une rencontre loin de l'Hôtel de Ville* (2004), *Juste une petite valse* (2000), and *L'Attraction du bal* (1987). Fleischman died in Paris on 15 July 2010 and is buried in the Bagneux cemetery. In an irony he would have appreciated, that was the setting of his story "Vanité," which appears in *France: A Traveler's Literary Companion* (Whereabouts Press, 2008).

prised, so thrilled, that he gave the issue away for free and paid the association's treasurer for it out of his own pocket. When he left the hall, he found the magazine discarded on the sidewalk. He bent down and picked it up, furious, and noticed that three or four pages had been torn out. The guy who did it was busy wiping snow off the windows of his car with them. He even had the chutzpah to tip his hat when he spotted Preverman and shout to him, "See, your magazine's really useful today!"

Ever since that evening, whenever there was a talk, Preverman would lay out an assortment of Yiddish records and corned beef sandwiches on the table for when the reading was over.

The organizers of the various associations that contacted him were surprised by his selling food. Records, they might understand, perhaps, but not sandwiches! They were wrong, though, because the music didn't sell any better than the literary works. On the other hand, the corned beef really took off. And so he quite naturally got into the habit of settling down behind his table at ten thirty, after the reading, perfectly at ease. People would come over to him, they'd get a sandwich, and talk.

Soon he completely abandoned the records with his poems set to music and interpreted by a female singer. He would only sell one of them now and then, whereas if he put out thirty or so corned beef sandwiches, they would disappear.

Of course, the associations and clubs didn't consider it appropriate. But since their speakers' fees weren't very high, they let it go. Yiddish cuisine could also offer cultural insight—except that he wasn't promoting cuisine but merely selling plain, run-of-the-mill corned beef sandwiches.

In May (he'd started selling them in December), Preverman announced to a woman who'd invited him to a reading that he no longer wanted to speak but that he would gladly attend the event "just for the sandwiches." She laughed and went along with it, thinking he was kidding. But indeed, two weeks later, he spoke only a few words.

"Dear friends," he began, "a big thank you to everyone for coming here. I've prepared something special."

The audience approved.

He continued, "Today I have the pleasure, the privilege, and the opportunity to present to all in attendance a marvel: a corned beef sandwich that's not only still mostly hot, not only with two slices of pickle but also with *chrain*—horseradish—that the great poet Tchernichovsky himself would have enjoyed! Ladies and gentlemen," he continued solemnly, "it is now time for me to step aside. I will serve them myself."

Amid scattered applause, Preverman pulled a large suitcase out from under the podium and headed toward the lobby to spread the sandwiches out on a table.

People looked at each other, and a few of them got up.

Since a great orator, a poet, had said it was something special, one could only believe him. Soon the thirty people in the hall followed Preverman out to the lobby, where he gave change with one hand while holding out a sandwich wrapped in waxed paper with the other.

Business was brisk that evening and after they'd eaten, people asked him questions, which extended the soiree.

He was considered unquestionably the best poet of his generation, and a good time was had by all.

By now, he was organizing a gathering every week.

Wurstag, the butcher who supplied the meat, could hardly complain. In fact, he asked Preverman what was going on. Preverman explained the situation and offered to bring him along one evening. Wurstag declined, wiping his hands on his apron. But one Sunday in June he decided he'd like to go after all.

Preverman gave his usual speech. He was about to invite everyone to step out and have a sandwich when Wurstag raised his hand. Preverman nodded to him and announced, "Tonight, we have here with us our friend Wurstag."

A few people clapped.

"Excuse me," the butcher began. "I'm not used to speaking in public, but I wanted to say that it's a real pleasure to be of service to a great poet like Monsieur Preverman."

The audience applauded more loudly.

Wurstag continued, "A great honor, it is. Truly. To share the stage with the genius who wrote,

A man is a man,
A poet is a poet . . . "

He then began to recite, in Yiddish, Preverman's famous poem.

This went on for ten minutes. It was beautiful, and everyone applauded.

Wurstag looked over at Preverman, whose brow was furrowed. Thinking the recitation pleased him, Wurstag launched into another great poem—one that had been set to music, but which he recited valiantly.

It was a decent success. There was a ripple of applause, which then petered out.

Wurstag felt encouraged to go on. Behind the podium,

Preverman desperately gestured for him to sit down. The butcher didn't understand and switched to a hymn that the poet had composed in 1950.

With his suitcase of sandwiches stashed under the podium, Preverman grew more and more annoyed. The butcher was massacring his words. Unable to bear it any longer, Preverman got up and, in unison with Wurstag, strove to declaim his text with the proper accent and intonation. This impromptu duo had the audience in stitches. When both had finished—together, this time—the room was roaring. Everyone rose to their feet, clapping wildly. Preverman wiped his forehead with his handkerchief. Not insensitive to the applause, he took a modest bow.

"Dear friends, encouraged by your warm reception . . . "

He hesitated; the applause had tapered off a bit but instantly resumed. He gestured for silence and then continued.

"By popular demand, I am going to . . . "

He glanced at his feet and saw the suitcase.

"I'm going to show you . . . "

Preverman tried hard to think of something new to offer, since the sandwiches had already had their day.

Just in case, however, he called out, "But first, we'll have a five-minute intermission! Mr. Wurstag, the butcher from rue Roi-de-Sicile whom you've all applauded, will come by with his sandwiches."

He gestured to Wurstag, who joined him on stage, and handed him the suitcase.

Wurstag took it, opened it, and started distributing the sandwiches.

When the butcher had sold the last one, he signaled from

across the room that the suitcase was empty, so they could now continue.

Preverman rose. He stood up on his chair and started shrinking. He got smaller and smaller and smaller . . . Then he leaped onto the green carpet that covered the stage and settled on a piece of paper that was lying there. The sheet curled up around him as if he were a slice of bread with corned beef.

The audience couldn't comprehend what was going on.

Wurstag thought he sort of understood. He came up from the back of the room to collect this last forgotten sandwich. Without looking too closely, he slipped off the paper and began eating it, automatically, while waiting for the speaker to return.

Preverman didn't hold it against him. He'd run out of ideas for how to earn his living as a poet.

Translated by Rose Vekony

The Armoire

Pascal Garnier

THE ARMOIRE filled Obsolète's whole window. It was a beautiful piece of furniture and the antique store owner must have been proud of it, to put it front and center and risk overshadowing all the other objects around it. The light wood gleamed like satin, and the armoire's proportions were simple and clean, with no rococo carving to weigh it down. It so perfectly framed Gabriel's reflection in the store window, it could have been made for him. The open door made you want to step inside. No coffin could be more comfortable. Crossing through eternity would become a cruise.

"Eight hundred euros, you say?"

"It's solid cherry. All mortise and tenon joints. Not a nail or a screw in it."

PASCAL GARNIER (1949–2010) was a widely published mystery writer with a gift for creating memorable characters in often-drab surroundings. His many books include *Comment va la douleur?* (2006), *Parenthèse* (2004), and *Les Hauts du bas* (2003). The following excerpt is from his 2008 novel *La Théorie du panda*.

"So it's edible?"

"Beg pardon?"

"You can eat it. It doesn't contain any metal, right?"

"I don't understand."

"No matter. It's really beautiful. Thank you."

Too bad Mathieu was dead. Gabriel would've liked to have bought it for him. Mathieu had eaten an armoire, the one his wife died in. She'd been suffocated by her furs when the door accidentally closed on her. Mathieu had been hopelessly in love with his wife. Wild with grief, he held the piece of furniture responsible and swore that he would eat it, right down to its last leg. It had taken him years, but chip by chip, splinter by splinter, he had devoured the entire thing. Every morning, he would cut off a piece with a pocketknife and chew it with the tenacity that only a thwarted love could sustain. The armoire was a mahogany Louis Philippe. In just two years he had already eaten a door.

"See, Gabriel, the problem is the hinges. The mahogany goes down fine, but the hinges don't. That's what makes a Louis Philippe such a drag."

But the desire for revenge can only last so long. Though Mathieu would never admit it, the hatred he felt for the armoire gradually turned into the same all-consuming love he felt for his gentle wife. He was now eating the object of his resentment like a gourmet.

"Yesterday I boiled up a piece of the frame. You would have thought it was veal!"

One night Mathieu phoned, in tears.

"Gabriel, I finished it. Come over."

Mathieu lay stretched out on his bed. He was very skinny. He hadn't eaten anything except wood since making that fatal promise, and despite what they say, mahogany isn't very nourishing. The only sign of the armoire were the dents its feet had left on the dusty floor and a massive silhouette on the faded wallpaper.

"She was a good one, you know . . . "

Translated by William Rodarmor

Roll On, Camembert

Jacques Perret

ON AN OCTOBER EVENING in Honfleur, Collot and I decided to haul the boat out at low tide below the main harbor basin. We wanted to scrape the hull and put on a coat of antifouling paint. If you're a sailor, it's always a good idea to take a look down there from time to time, to see what's happening under the waterline. You never know. Without your realizing it, the boat may be dragging a monster with suckers, a caulk-munching triton, a mass of Sargasso weed, a colony of pearl oysters, a helping of winkles, an old impaled swordfish, or maybe a litter of baby sea monkeys clinging to

---

JACQUES PERRET (1901–1992) was a French writer best known for his 1947 novel *Le Caporal épinglé*. It tells the story of his captivity in Germany and of his escape attempts, and was made into a film (*The Elusive Corporal*) by director Jean Renoir in 1962. Perret was also nominated for an Academy Award for Best Story for the film *The Sheep Has Five Legs* (1954). This excerpt is from *Rôle de plaisance*, a 1957 memoir about Perret's adventures aboard his wooden yawl *Matam* with his friend and sailing partner, Collot.

the maternal hull. Remember, a sailboat is a living thing, and everything alive has its share of mystery. So we sailed *Matam* from the Honfleur basin into the lower harbor, so we would be ready to transit to the tidal zone the next morning.

We were lucky enough to be able to tie up at the dock next to a ladder. It was getting toward dinnertime, and we decided to walk into town to buy some groceries. But first we slacked off on our mooring lines, because the tide was already ebbing. Collot and I had been sailing long enough to be past that point where, coming back from having a drink, you find your boat hanging from the dock six feet above the water.

You know what running errands can be like, though. You meet people, they buy you a round, you return the favor, and time passes. But in this case our conscience was eased by the knowledge that as the tide ebbed, the boat would be gently settling into the mud. Honfleur mud is exceptionally soft and very gentle with wooden hulls. It has thousands of stories from the old days to tell, because harbor mud has a prodigious memory. *Matam* wouldn't be bored, so we could drink a few extra glasses of muscadet with a clear conscience.

At nightfall on the way back, we could see that the tide had gone out. But what we could make out of our boat in the darkness was less than satisfactory. Instead of settling squarely into the mud, as she usually did, *Matam* was lying sprawled on her port side, at an angle of 45 degrees, maybe 46. When you see somebody else's boat in a situation like that, a boat that means nothing to you, it merely suggests comfortable ease and laziness. But when it's your own boat, your imagination works differently. You start asking yourself questions. You even wonder if the boat's hapless position might not spell something worse.

Whatever the case, when we climbed on board we immediately understood that the evening would be less pleasant than we'd imagined. First, we stated several times and in different ways that there was no danger to the boat itself. The mud was quite soft and though *Matam* hadn't settled properly, that was no problem; she would be afloat as soon as the tide came in. We then decided to cook dinner as if nothing was out of the ordinary.

That resolution wasn't easy to keep, because the now slanted universe could hardly go unnoticed by two men like Collot and me, who were accustomed to a vertical existence. The surface normally reserved for feet could no longer be used. If the boat had been lying squarely on her side, we could have stood on the closets. And if she had been completely upside down, we could have easily walked on the ceiling, because a world that is totally upside down is much more livable than a world that is somewhat at an angle. At sea, the rolling and pitching had long ago taught us the essential fragility of all the horizontal lines aboard, of course. But here we were frozen in disequilibrium, trapped off center, immobilized aslant.

We first tried clinging to the slope, out of an instinctive loyalty to the floor. But a floor is no longer worthy of the name when it starts to tilt, and we weren't about to spend the night on board like a pair of mountain climbers in distress, dangling from a cliff. It might occur to you that we could just go sleep at a hotel, but sorry, no; that simply isn't done.

We finally located the precious verticality so essential to our equilibrium at the angle where the boat's ribs and keel boards meet, and where universal gravity now passed through. But because the human foot isn't designed to walk at an angle, we adopted a sitting position. Yielding to gravity, we initially crouched gingerly against the port side of the hull, but our combined weight made the boat lean further. While again reassuring each other that there was absolutely no risk to the hull, we scaled the slope to settle on the starboard side. We sat parked on the edge of the bunk, our legs tensed to keep from sliding. In that position, we now contemplated dinner.

Needless to say, all the objects aboard had undergone similar perturbations, but they had opted to uncomplainingly join the incongruous situation. We were therefore confronted with a fait accompli. The dishes, for example, had burst from the cupboard to scatter to new, totally inappropriate locations and settle there. We, on the other hand, couldn't be expected to adapt to the a-skewering of man's natural condition just like that. One by one, we were forced to revise all the learned notions and gestures acquired in a society founded on respect for the perpendicular and optical illusion.

An evil-minded reader might now insinuate that the muscadet we had drunk could be related to these upheavals, but that would be indulging in gratuitous slander while avoiding the real issue. Serious thinkers of a scientific bent, on the other hand, will understand perfectly when I stress that our disorientation persisted because we lacked any reference point. The boat's hatch was closed, so we had no way to refer to the perspectives of the outside world. We were caught, trapped in an aberration yet victims of an upbringing that kept us from surrendering to it. Theoretically, the lamp hanging from the ceiling should have illustrated orthodox verticality, but the sight of it was so unsettling that we preferred not to look.

It was under those conditions that we prepared to cook some onion soup. We set our little stove on a wooden board that we assumed was properly horizontal, and were thunderstruck to see the water spill out of the pot on the one side we least expected it to. Collot straightened the stove and covered the pot with a plate to spare us this unsettling sight. The plate promptly slipped off, and we would have sworn it should have slid in the other direction. Our appetite was poor. You can't eat a hearty meal when surrounded by the collapse of the three dimensions that have sustained you since childhood.

The smell of the onion soup may have affected the state of the things around us, because an absolutely extraordinary phenomenon then occurred. We had cooked the soup with relative success on the wooden board. Collot now straightened the board and set the camembert on it. For some reason, my friend put the round container on edge, rather than flat. No sooner had he released it than we watched with stupefaction as the cheese rolled up the board. To silence any naysayers, let me say right away that the cheese was perfectly edible. What was involved was a major challenge to the established laws of physics. The camembert climbed the slope steadily, smoothly accelerating, exactly as it would have descended it in a normal world. From that moment on, we were ready for anything.

Translated by William Rodarmor

Pique-Nique

Dominique Sylvain

INGRID DIESEL had almost finished giving Michèle Las-tret her massage, but couldn't bear to let her leave. Michèle's story had started Ingrid daydreaming, and she wanted to hear all the details.

"Alain and I are taking the Eurostar this evening," she said. "Christopher will be waiting for us at the station, and we'll head straight into the country. We're taking the good-ies in our luggage. We've got Champagne, rillettes and ter-rines, macaroons, and my special chocolate cake with sea salt crystals. And I've found the most amazing evening gown."

After Michèle left, Ingrid braved the rain to join Lola

DOMINIQUE SYLVAIN (1957–) is an award-winning French thriller writer, with over a dozen titles to her name. She now lives in Tokyo. In 2004 she launched a mystery series featuring a crime-solving foodie odd couple in Paris: the tall, blond, American massage therapist Ingrid Diesel (think Uma Thurman), and the short, dark, retired police detective Lola Jost (think Kathy Bates). This story appeared in Sylvain's 2008 collection *Régals du Japon et d'ailleurs*.

Jost for lunch at their favorite bistro, Belles de jour comme de nuit. She found the former *commissaire de police* sitting on the terrace with a blanquette de veau and a glass of Sancerre. Lola offered Ingrid some wine, but she refused.

"I'd just *love* to dress up in an evening gown and go for a picnic in the English countryside and listen to Mozart," Ingrid confessed.

Lola looked at her American friend's khaki tank top and shredded jeans and refrained from comment. She topped up her glass instead.

"Do you realize that Michèle and Alain are going off to England to have a picnic and listen to opera?" Ingrid went on. "It's a garden party that only happens once a year. The guests put on tuxedos, they bring out the good china, the big wicker picnic baskets, and those soft travel blankets to sit on. The English really know how to preserve their charming customs."

"You're not telling me anything new," said Lola, "I was married to one of them. He never took me on a picnic with Mozart in the background, though. Do you want some blanquette? Maxime really nailed it this time."

"Maxime nails everything he tries his hand at," Ingrid said with a sigh.

"What's the matter? Rain getting you down?"

Ingrid shrugged and ordered a ham sandwich and mineral water.

Lola looked on unruffled as this spartan meal arrived, then finished her blanquette. When the coffee was served, she had an idea.

"We'll have a picnic in the Parc Monceau this evening. You wear a dress, morning or evening, just as you please, and

I'll bring my CD player. We'll ask Maxime to put together a fantastic picnic for us."

"But it's raining, Lola."

"Haven't you noticed that the sky has been clearing by early evening these last few days?"

"You think?"

"And I'm considering making an unexpected phone call to one of my classiest connections."

"*Qui ça?*"

"Commissaire Serge Clémenti. He has a touch of salt-of-the-earth about him, a bit British."

"He's English?"

"Absolutely not."

"A good-looking guy," said Ingrid. "I remember we met him on a café terrace."

"Now you're with me, great."

"But Clémenti will never accept an invitation to a picnic at short term."

"It's short *notice*, Ingrid. And Clémenti's not averse to a bit of eccentricity. Quite the opposite, in fact."

Lola vigorously waved away her friend's remaining objections and went off to the kitchen to order a gourmet picnic. Then she announced that it was time to get back to their respective occupations: a ten-thousand-piece puzzle for her, a series of massage appointments for Ingrid. As Lola exited, she called out: "Rendezvous for an amazing English picnic, Parc Monceau, around six o'clock!" Ingrid watched her substantial silhouette moving down the covered passage towards the Saint-Denis neighborhood behind a curtain of driving rain. A few minutes later, she saw her coming back.

"*Que diable!?* You look awful, Lola."

"I bumped into a corpse. Come and see."

The masseuse obediently followed the former cop. Lola pointed at a carpet, tied with string, soaking up the rain on the sidewalk. Two men were busy loading stuff into a hired van.

"You've overcooked it on the Sancerre, Lola!"

"We say *overdone* it on the wine. And overcooked the dinner."

"Somebody's just moving their stuff."

"That's not what Sigmund thinks."

What could their psychoanalyst friend's dog have to do with anything? Ingrid wondered.

"When I saw Sigmund straining at his leash to sniff that rug, I thought—"

"That there was a body inside it? And the body would go unnoticed in a fake house moving?"

"Exactly."

"*C'est fou!*"

Ingrid protested, but Lola wouldn't let go of the idea. She was determined to shadow the movers and put *them* on the carpet to get at the truth. Ingrid told her she was giving the drycleaner from rue de Lancry a Balinese massage at two o'clock. Lola promised to call if there were any developments.

Lola borrowed Maxime's van and settled behind the steering wheel to wait until the suspects left. She had time to call Clémenti and invite him to their impromptu picnic. Her wait was disturbed by a tapping on the windshield. Ingrid slid onto the passenger seat and announced she had put off her appointments. Lola gave her an affectionate smile.

"And I took a peek into the apartment the fake movers are working in," Ingrid continued, looking conspiratorial.

"I didn't even see you!"

"You were on the phone," said Ingrid. "I asked a neighbor. She says it's a third floor apartment, a young guy called Philippe Montserrat. A feed writer. The move has been planned for ages. Monsieur Monserrat let the movers in and . . ."

"Not a *feed* writer, a food writer. Did you speak to the man?"

"No, the living room is empty and the tenant has disappeared."

"I knew it! Are you sure they didn't spot you?"

"Positive."

The two men drove off in the van. Lola slipped into their wake as they headed onto the *périphérique*, then exited at Aubervilliers. The driver parked in front of a rundown apartment building. Lola parked too, a hundred yards farther on. She listened to the weather report—no unsettled weather predicted for Paris and the surrounding area—then turned off the ignition.

"By the way, I called Clémenti," Lola said as they walked toward the building.

"Is he up for it?"

"Affirmative, and he remembers you."

"*Vraiment?* That's unbelievable."

"Not really. You often have that effect on men, eccentrics or not."

The two movers had just unloaded the carpet and were entering the building. Ingrid and Lola went into the stairwell, which was littered with garbage and used syringes. A not unpleasant smell of fish hung in the air. The door to the second-floor apartment was open. They could hear a conversation between two men and a woman.

"What's to eat?"

"Cod with steamed potatoes," the woman snapped.

"Not my favorite," the other man growled.

"You see me making like Bocuse in this dump? Consider yourselves lucky. You got the guy?"

"He's in the carpet."

"So what are you waiting for? Get him out of there."

"First we eat, then we untie him. Paul Mercurion wants us to scare the shit out of him, see."

'No names, you jerk!"

"With the dose we gave him, no way he'll hear us."

"Unwrap him and tie him to the radiator. Is he blind-folded?"

"Taped up nice and tight."

Lola decided it was time to alert Lieutenant Jérôme Bathélemy, her former assistant at the 10th arrondissement police headquarters. She signaled to Ingrid, and the two friends tiptoed down the stairs. In the van, Lola explained the whole setup to Barthélemy, who promised to come immediately.

"Paul Mercurion . . . The name seems familiar, Lola."

"He's a well-known chef. And according to Maxime, he's totally paranoid."

They were interrupted by a sudden explosion of glass. Ingrid swore when she saw the fake moving men standing by their shattered windshield. Each was clutching a baseball bat.

"Get out of there!" roared the bigger of the two. "Or we'll rearrange your faces!"

The two women stood with their hands up in the middle of the deserted street. It was as empty as the rest of this charming neighborhood, Lola realized.

They were marched up the stairs and made to sit on a couch that smelled of dust mites, next to an obviously drugged man handcuffed to a radiator. The fake movers and their cook ate their cod in silence. When the meal was over, the more nervous of the men slapped Ingrid in the face and started to question her. Lola got a pair of good hard slaps for protesting. Then Ingrid got a third, for trying to support her friend.

"Tell us who you're working for, Yankee, or I'll scald you with the milk we used to poach the cod."

Ingrid launched into a realistically detailed story starring Paul Mercurion and his British equivalent, the famous chef Julian Christie. The London chef specialized in organizing elegant garden parties in the English countryside, she explained, and all the gentry knew of his excellent reputation. Christie had called in the private detective company she and Lola worked for. He was planning to go into partnership with Mercurion but first he wanted to know what he was getting into.

"Into a nice little ratatouille," Lola continued, delighted that her friend had whipped up a story that was long enough to give Barthélemy time to come to the rescue.

And in fact, when the lieutenant and three of his men showed up, they did a credible imitation of a SWAT team. The baseball bats and cod-poaching milk were no match for the cops' Berettas.

"In Paul Mercurion's restaurant, Le Château bleu, they can't tell chic from chichi. Take the snail soup served under a layer of mashed potatoes. They're aiming for traditional country-style food, but all they achieve is grotesque. Creativity should be limited by common sense . . ."

Serge Clémenti listened closely as Lola read. He was holding a glass of Champagne in one hand, and his black tuxedo contrasted sharply with the green wicker chair and lawn. Wearing a gown as golden as the sunset, her short blond curls molded into sweet little spikes by the most fantastic hair gel, Ingrid was slicing the vegetable basil terrine. Lola finished reading Philippe Montserrat's review from the June issue of *Emotion Cuisine* and smiled with satisfaction.

"So if I've got this right," said Clémenti, "this young food writer took a swipe at Paul Mercurion, and Mercurion decided to teach him a good, hard lesson, anonymously."

"That's it exactly, Serge. He planned to keep Montserrat in some rat hole for a while, feeding him nothing but chocolate-flavored baby food. Over the last few years, Mercurion has been less and less tolerant of criticism. When he found out Montserrat was moving, he set up a fairly cunning kidnapping—by sending the fake movers before the real ones."

"Cunning? I don't think so. More overly contrived, like his food. Montserrat summed him up pretty well, actually."

"Anyway, none of that spoiled our picnic," said Ingrid.

"This was a terrific idea. What made you think of it?"

"Well, this morning as I was massaging one of my clients, I realized I'd love to picnic in an evening gown in the English countryside, listening to Mozart."

"But we're not in England," he said. "And what happened to Mozart?"

"Crap! I forgot the CD player!" said Lola.

No problem, thought Ingrid, as she and Clémenti exchanged lingering looks.

Translated by Jean Anderson

Sweet Nothings

Christiane Baroche

YOU KNOW THOSE PEOPLE who stop you in the street and ask stupid questions, like they're taking a poll, or try to make you act like a fool for a hidden camera? Playing games, right? Everybody's playing games, these days. Well, playing—that's easy to say. Turn on the TV, you'll see it all: they've got your age, your mother-in-law's age, the date you filed your first income tax return (maybe to haul you in for an audit). Everybody's playing to win. It gets on my nerves, let me tell you.

Okay, so I'm at the corner of rue Soufflot and rue Victor-Cousin, and this little guy with a beard, looks like he's fifty but he's broke and doing community service, asks me who I'm gonna vote for, and what I do in life. I say pal, I'm voting for retirement, and if you really want to know, I'm a cop.

CHRISTIANE BAROCHE (1935–) is a French novelist, short story writer, and poet. She won the 1978 Prix Goncourt for her novel *Chambres, avec vue sur le passé*. This story is from her 1990 collection, *Giocoso, ma non . . .*

Under a confidentiality agreement, know what that means? I vote for whoever my wallet tells me to vote for.

After all, I wasn't about to tell him the whole story, how I got fired without any kind of due process just because I laughed at the wrong moment. Really takes the cake, doesn't it?

In any case, the guy gets the hell out of there. He was sure I was gonna ask for his papers and bust him for misdemeanor curiosity.

Crazy, how much I thought about the whole thing afterward! I keep telling myself that retirement's hard, whether it's close or far, and I was only two years away anyway. Still, I can't get used to it. Especially since everybody felt like laughing that day, even the guy in question. Well, it seems I shouldn't have laughed, or at least not been the first. If the division chief had set the tone, then it would have been okay to chime in, of course. Same old story.

Want me to tell you about it? 'Cause I've got all the time in the world, man! I can give you details, keep you guessing! It's not just the Americans and the little guy with the glass eye and the shabby raincoat who can keep you in suspense. My old lady claims I never know how to tell stories, but what she likes is whatever's happening somewhere else, like Miami, which looks a lot richer than Seine-Saint-Denis, for sure! And then there's Mannix on TV . . . Okay, I'm fatter than he is, and I don't have as much hair or as many teeth (actually I've got the same number, but when I see him, I always feel like he's got a whole mouthful). Plus I don't have some handy millionaire to shake down for sticking his hand up the wrong skirt, or to whack over an oil deal gone bad. No, my story's real simple, just an ordinary stickup. I'm sure that numbskull must've seen an Alain Delon thriller the day before. Except he shows up *after* the armored car has picked up the money. Some people just don't have any luck.

It happened in a pissant Banque CIC branch, a hole in the wall out in the *péiphérique* suburbs. The Brink's truck comes by right after the indoor market closes. That's because the stallholders empty their cash boxes before they take off; they don't want to shlep their money around all day Sunday, see. And the head of the bank doesn't want to leave the funds from the three SuperInterMammouthExtra stores sitting in his safe; human nature, right?

So my guy shows up half an hour late. He's pale as an endive, and he sticks a gun under fat Madame Beulemans's nose. He's shaking so much, everybody's scared. The teller says to herself, When he sees I don't have anything to give him, or practically nothing, he's going to shoot me. She starts to cry, "I've just got a few francs, m'sieur, that's all I can give you, I swear."

There isn't even anybody in the lobby to take hostage. I'm telling you, we're really at the tail end of the afternoon!

The guy's standing there like a jerk, mouth open, waving his gun around. "I'm not asking for the moon or what's in the safe," he stammers. "I just want a little dough, please." When the accounts manager hears this—he's a young guy who's trying to pass for a Wall Street raider (the harm TV does! *Apocalypse Now* even out in the countryside, imagine!), he's thin, wears pure imitation Dior ties, only he's got the cheeks of a choirboy, so he isn't fooling anybody. So this young guy—drives a GT bought from the want ads and wears Mexican boots on Sunday, I've seen them . . . Okay,

I'm digressing, but I'm trying to give you the whole picture, it matters.

Anyway, the young guy walks over to the teller to say to keep calm, and he pushes the button that connects the bank to the station. Thirty seconds later, we're there.

High drama. The place is sealed off, there's cops and detectives everywhere, the division chief's got a megaphone. We're even given a sharpshooter: little Pinson, the French clay-pigeon champion. I don't know if that's the right name of the thing he does—trick shooting, I think. Trapshooting? You sure? Yeah, okay. Whatever.

You got to admit, it's a great scene. To think we get accused of not having a sense of humor. Pinson's never shot at anything in his life except dinner plates, and he's shitting bricks at having to aim his rifle at a real person. (Pinson's a good little guy, by the way. He volunteers at soup kitchens when his father isn't looking.)

Needless to say, there's lots of people at the windows. It's better than TV, practically live. And of course there's always someone to yell, "Kill him!" or "Fuck the pigs!" They're scoping out the sidewalk for fresh blood, and they're always happy to see some cop slip on a banana peel. Whatever. People are who they are, and their shoes don't get shined every day.

While we're being deployed according to Division Chief Petiot's orders, the scene inside the bank is playing out with no commercial breaks. "Since that's the way things are," mumbles our kid gangster, "I'm leaving." Verbatim.

The poor guy comes out, and he falls into our arms like a ripe cherry.

Petiot raises his finger, and Pinson uncurls his, with a big sigh of relief. We all look at each other, and we feel kind of stupid. A whole regiment of idiots in costume, with bulletproof vests, shields, grenade launchers. There's even an ambulance with a gurney and oxygen, and a dozen firefighters in full regalia: axes, fire extinguishers, rope ladders, crowbars, the whole nine yards.

We fall back in good order, without drums or bugles, but with a sour taste in our mouths. 'Cause we recognized the guy. His name's Laval, and he's been coming to the unemployment office for a while, but his benefits are running out. We're none too happy to see him, me even less than the others.

A little later, I "abandoned common sense and laughed inappropriately," according to the chief, who had it in for me anyway. Petiot, who was in a foul mood—in front of the bank, someone had yelled, "Hey Petiot, your chimney's smoking. Is it your mother-in-law?"—Petiot, who's got a poker up his ass, has been warning the guy, telling him what he was going to get for robbing a bank. Aggravated, he says. The poor slob just shrugs, as if to say things are already bad enough, how could they get any worse?

"Armed robbery, that'll get you twenty years!"

Then the guy puts his hand in his pocket, and we all freeze. We just realized that nobody had disarmed him . . .

"Take it easy, Laval."

Laval, that moron, is looking at us as if we're telling him about the attack on Fort Knox, with the right gestures, even!

He takes his hand out of his pocket, holding his gun by the barrel.

A Magnum! We can hardly believe our eyes. We can hear

Pinson cock his rifle and his teeth chattering, and we come really close to being the news story of the year!

Laval is staring at us in amazement, and then he starts looking scared to death. We're looking back at him real nasty like.

And that's when I laughed. I know, I shouldn't have, but my eyes are too sharp, what can I say? I laughed before anybody else did, and that was my error, as Petiot would say. 'Cause the poor guy doesn't shoot, see. Far from it. He starts to eat his gun. The gun is made of nougat candy.

See, you don't think it's funny either. But I wasn't laughing stupidly; I was relieved, that's all. The whole drama had just been a farce.

Everybody agreed about that, of course. Only I should've laughed according to the chain of command, as it were.

Anyway, I'm not the one in the story you should feel sorry for. I still have friends—cops of course; we don't know a lot of other people. Besides, who wants a cop for a friend? People are always saying that pulling on a blue suit with a badge would be the last thing they'd think of doing, but people like that, they've never been on unemployment. As for me, what can I say? I'm just not given to carving Magnums out of nougat.

Don't get me wrong, I'm not judging anybody. I go see Laval in Fresnes Prison from time to time. I bring him oranges, tobacco, decks of cards, whatever. Someday, when a lot of water has flowed under the bridge and through our lives, I'll bring him some nougat. If he laughs, it means he's past the worst. I hope so, anyway. Although I doubt it; Laval hasn't hit bottom yet. I know what I'm talking about. His troubles began when he married my daughter. She's not half stupid, either; she's totally dumb. I could tell the moment she was born. She was a strange baby: when she nursed, she didn't suck, she blew!

All right. When I say Laval hasn't hit bottom yet . . . At my last visit, that asshole asked me for some black soap. He probably wants to carve another gun, play double or nothing. With his luck, it'll be raining that day, so of course he'll be caught again. And this time, instead of eating his gun, he can use it to wash his hands.

Believe me, I won't even crack a smile. You can fool me once, but not twice.

In the end, it's kind of a sad story, don't you think?

Translated by William Rodarmor

Pralines

Roger Grenier

"OLD MONSIEUR ALBAN will be making pralines next Thursday."

"Think I could go watch, Papa?"

"Yes. He invited you over, which is why I'm mentioning it."

"Good thing he's making the pralines on Thursday,"

When the day came, Jean-Baptiste's father said to him: "You haven't forgotten that old Monsieur Alban is making pralines today, have you?"

"No. What time should I go?"

ROGER GRENIER (1919–) is a prize-winning author, journalist, and radio personality. As a young man, he studied with philosopher Gaston Bachelard and worked with Albert Camus on the staff of *Combat*. In 1985, he was awarded the Grand Prix of the Académie française for his body of work, whose thirty-odd books include *Les Larmes d'Ulysse* (1998, tr. *The Difficulty of Being a Dog*), and two best sellers: *Ciné-roman* (1972) and *Le Palais d'hiver* (1965). This story is from his 1982 collection *La Fiancée de Fragonard*.

"Two o'clock. I bet you won't be able to go there all by yourself."

"Why do you say that?"

"You're a little shy, and I always felt that old Monsieur Alban scared you."

"He looks like Clemenceau."

"See, he scares you."

"Well, he invited me, after all."

"Listen, I'm going to come with you."

"You don't have to."

"Sure I do."

When the time came, Jean-Baptiste's father put his salespeople in charge of the jewelry store.

"I have an errand to run with the kid," he said.

He led his son through the streets of the town to a store near the cathedral. It sold postcards, souvenirs, and of course plaster and gilt models of the cathedral itself, exact replicas of the monument that was the pride of the town. In the back of the store stood a woman with brown hair and very red lips.

"Here we are," said Jean-Baptiste's father.

"Hello, Madame Alban," the boy said.

"How big he's gotten!"

"You think so? He'll do his first communion next year."

"So soon! But he still looks so young. Every year, when they all come out in procession on the forecourt across the way, I just can't help it. I get tears in my eyes. So much innocence, and then life . . . "

"Isn't your salesgirl here yet?"

"No, she seems to be running late."

"Yeah. I wonder why."

"I hope she comes."

"So do I."

Madame Alban sat down on the tall stool behind the cash register. She stretched out a leg and her thigh muscles played under her tight beige jersey dress. Jean-Baptiste's father came over, almost close enough to touch her. No one said anything and the boy wondered what they were waiting for. Maybe for the salesgirl to come?

After a long moment, Madame Alban said: "I'll take the boy upstairs to my father-in-law's. Charles, would you mind watching the store for a moment?"

She slid down from the stool. The boy was so fascinated by the movement and the metamorphoses of her red lips that he paid no attention to the meaning of the words.

"Come along!" she had to say, opening her scarlet mouth one last time.

"Can you get home by yourself?" asked Jean-Baptiste's father.

"Yes."

"I'll pick you up if I swing by here."

Madame Alban led the boy through the back of the store. She opened a door, and they found themselves in a courtyard where an outside staircase led to old Monsieur Alban's rooms. He was a retired candy maker and he liked to dust off his old skills a few times a year. Madame Alban knocked, then opened the door. Her perfume, which Jean-Baptiste had been breathing in while following her up the stairs, was suddenly replaced by that of sugar beginning to caramelize. The retired candy maker was wearing an apron and had already begun his preparations. Jean-Baptiste once again thought that his head looked like Clemenceau's, the Father of Victory.

"I'm bringing you the kid. He's wanted to see you work for such a long time. He's very well behaved, won't be any bother."

"Okay. Is Maurice downstairs? I haven't seen him yet today."

"You know he's spending all day at the commercial court."

"Oh, that's right. So who's minding the store? Is the girl here already?"

"Yes."

No she isn't, you're mistaken, Jean-Baptiste almost said. But he had been taught that even in this polite form, you mustn't accuse grownups of lying. She just doesn't want to worry her father-in-law, he thought. It's quicker to say yes, it avoids endless explanations. He knew the trick, having practiced it often himself.

"I'm going downstairs now. I'll let you work. Mmm . . . It smells good in here. You're making me hungry."

"I've only just begun."

She left. You could hear her heels clattering down the steps. Jean-Baptiste remained with the old man in the kitchen, a dark room that had to be lit with an electric light. A copper pot already sat on the stove. The candy maker went over and looked at its contents severely. Without saying a word, he turned the gas down a little, picked up a spatula, and started stirring.

From the moment the old man leaned over the copper pot, time changed its rhythm and nature. It almost stopped flowing. It was like the thick syrup he was cooking. The boy stood motionless in a corner of the kitchen. There wasn't any place to sit.

Monsieur Alban abruptly left the stove and went to rummage in a box. He took handfuls of a powder and tossed it into the mixture he was cooking, then began to stir it again. Jean-Baptiste heard him muttering:

"I can't remember where Maurice went. He told me yesterday that he had something he had to do, but what? Losing your memory is so annoying!"

"Madame Alban said that he was at the commercial court," the boy said timidly.

But the old man didn't seem to be listening. He turned off the gas. He took the pot and poured its contents into a sifter, then shook the sifter over another pot. A kind of sand fell out of it, and Jean-Baptiste understood that this was cooked sugar. There were almonds left in the sifter. Monsieur Alban put them back in the pot and turned the gas on again. He leaned over the stove several times, adjusting the flame. It was always too high or too low. He never seemed satisfied. It was when he glared into the pots that he most looked like Clemenceau.

For a long time nothing happened, only the smell of the sugar and the almonds slowly cooking. Then the candy maker put some of the sugar he had cooked earlier back into the pot and ran everything through the sifter again. He didn't talk, only muttered to himself, so the boy didn't understand a thing about the sequence of the operations.

In the distance a Spanish song could be heard from a radio or a phonograph.

Ay, Dolores, Dolores . . .

Jean-Baptiste was bored. So this was it, making pralines?

Standing around without moving, watching a pot on the stove? But there was still the smell, which was marvelous and full of promise. The little boy started to think of things he would have preferred to forget: the arithmetic exercises he had for the next day; and geography: he could never remember the tributaries on the left bank of the Loire. He shifted from one foot to the other.

"Do you need to pee?" asked the old man.

"No."

You could still hear: *Ay, Dolores, Dolores . . .*

A second pot had joined the fray, with sugar that was already cooked, but this time with water in it. And then another pot, with more sugar and water, but also with gum arabic. Jean-Baptiste started thinking that it would've been more fun to be downstairs, playing with the little golden cathedrals that so wonderfully reproduced all of the details of the real one, or spinning the postcard display rack.

The praline-making operation now shifted away from the stove. The main theater of action was the table, on which a big sheet of zinc had been laid, as Jean-Baptiste only just now noticed. The old candy maker had picked up the pot of syrup and was tossing the hot almonds into it. He stirred it energetically, grumbling. The smell was more and more wonderful. Maybe the pralines would be ready soon. But the old man kept on stirring and stirring. At one point Jean-Baptiste thought he was finished, but Monsieur Alban picked up the second pot, emptied it into the first, and started stirring again, looking. This was never going to end.

The cruelest was yet to come, however. Monsieur Alban abruptly turned the pot over the zinc sheet and poured out what looked pretty much like pralines. They were finally done. The old man spread them out with a spatula, separating them. You probably had to wait for them to cool. It would be stupid to burn your tongue. Monsieur Alban began walking around, straightening up the kitchen, scraping and cleaning his pots. Tiny scraps of caramelized sugar had fallen near the edge of the table where Jean-Baptiste was standing. He furtively touched them with a damp fingertip and, with a falsely distracted look, put it in his mouth when the old man's back was turned. Meanwhile, he'd been staring at the pralines so long that he thought they looked like little skulls.

From behind, the old man leaning over his stove and his pots looked like a colossus. It seemed to take him forever to clean up, and Jean-Baptiste was annoyed at himself for not being more patient. Here he was, using his fingertip or nail to pick up tiny, ridiculous scraps within his reach, whereas in a few moments he would be eating real whole pralines, with their glaze, their crust of sugar, their perfectly grilled almond. He could feel himself salivating, like a dog.

There didn't seem to be anything left to put away in the kitchen. Monsieur Alban made an inspection tour, and Jean-Baptiste put his hands behind his back, looking guilty. When the old candy maker was finished examining everything, he went to get a large tin box. According to its faded, old-fashioned decoration, it had once held Huntley & Palmer cookies. He scooped up all the pralines with a spoon, dropped them into the tin, and closed the lid.

"I'm going to be leaving now," said Jean-Baptiste, his voice stretching out the final syllable.

"Yes, it's finished."

"Okay. Goodbye, monsieur."

The boy went downstairs into the courtyard. From there he took a hallway out to the street. But before going home he went into the souvenir store. Madame Alban was there, alone.

"Isn't my father here?" he asked her.

"No. You can see he isn't."

"He said he might come back to get me."

"Just go home before it gets too dark."

"Are you all alone? Didn't the salesgirl come?"

"No, she never came. I don't know what happened, and I had to watch the store all afternoon."

"You must have been bored."

"I'd planned to run some errands, and I wasn't able to."

"My father wanted to do some errands, too. Maybe that's why he didn't come back to pick me up."

"Run along home. It's getting late."

"All right. Good night, Madame Alban."

"Goodnight, sweetie."

When he got home, Jean-Baptiste found his father at the cash register, counting the receipts and looking glum.

"Good evening, Papa."

"Good evening. Did you have fun?"

"Not so much. It took a long time."

Jean-Baptiste wasn't sure he wanted to tell all about it. He remained standing in front of the cash register, looking at his father from below. I can't start crying over this, he thought to himself. But he felt so disappointed that he finally spoke up.

"You know, old Monsieur Alban had me watch him working for hours, and in the end he didn't even give me a single praline."

"You poor guy! See, there are days like that when you hope for things and nothing turns out the way you imagined it."

Then Jean-Baptiste's father added:

"You might not believe it, but in a certain way I didn't get any pralines today, either."

Translated by William Rodarmor

The Butcher

Alina Reyes

THE BLADE PLUNGED gently into the muscle then ran its full length in one supple movement. The action was perfectly controlled. The slice curled over limply onto the chopping block.

The black meat glistened, revived by the touch of the knife. The butcher placed his left hand flat on the broad rim and with his right hand began to carve into the thick meat once again. I could feel that cold elastic mass beneath the palm of my own hand. I saw the knife enter the firm dead flesh, opening it up like a shining wound. The steel blade slid down the length of the dark shape. The blade and the wall gleamed.

The butcher picked up the slices one after the other and

ALINA REYES (1956–) is a French writer best known for her literary treatment of eroticism. This excerpt is the first chapter of her notorious 1988 debut novel *Le Boucher*. It was published with *Lucie au Long Cours* (1990, tr. *Lucie's Long Voyage*) in *The Butcher and Other Erotica by* Grove Press. Both were translated by David Watson.

placed them side by side on the chopping block. They fell with a flat slap—like a kiss against the wood.

With the point of the knife the butcher began to dress the meat, cutting out the yellow fat and splattering it against the tiled wall. He ripped a piece of greaseproof paper from the wad hanging on the iron hook, placed a slice in the middle of it, dropped another on top. The kiss again, more like a clap.

Then he turned to me, the heavy packet flat on his hand, and he tossed it onto the scales.

The sickly smell of raw meat hit my nostrils. Seen close up, in the full summer morning light which poured in through the long window, it was bright red, beautifully nauseating. Who said that flesh is sad? Flesh is not sad, it is sinister. It belongs on the left side of our souls, it catches us at times of the greatest abandonment, carries us over deep seas, scuttles us and saves us; flesh is our guide, our dense black light, the well which draws our life down in a spiral, sucking it into oblivion.

The flesh of the bull before me was the same as that of the beast in the field, except that the blood had left it, the stream which carries life and carries it away so quickly, of which there remained only a few drops like pearls on the white paper.

And the butcher who talked to me about sex all day long was made of the same flesh, only warm, sometimes soft and sometimes hard; the butcher had his good and inferior cuts, exacting and eager to burn out their life, to transform themselves into meat. And my flesh was the same, I who felt the fire light between my legs at the butcher's words.

There was a slit along the bottom of the butcher's stall where he stuck his collection of knives for cutting, slicing and chopping. Before plunging one into the meat the butcher would sharpen the blade on his steel, running it up and down, first one side than the other, against the metal rod. The sharp scraping noise set my teeth on edge to their very roots.

The rabbits were hung behind the glass pane, pink, quartered, their stomachs opened to reveal their fat livers—exhibitionists, crucified martyrs, sacrificial offerings to covetous housewives. The chickens were suspended by the neck, their skinny yellow necks stretched and pierced by the iron hooks which held their heads pointed skywards; the fat bodies of poultry with grainy skin dangled wretchedly, with their whimsical parsons' noses stuck above their arseholes like the false noses on clowns' faces.

In the window, like so many precious objects, the different cuts of pork, beef and lamb were displayed to catch the eye of the customer. Fluctuating between pale pink and deep red, the joints caught the light like living jewels. Then there was the offal, the glorious offal, the most intimate, the most authentic, the most secretly evocative part of the deceased animal: flabby, dark, blood-red livers; huge, obscenely coarse tongues; enigmatic brains; kidneys coiled around their full girth; hearts tubed with veins—and those kept hidden in the fridge: the lights for granny's cat because they are too ugly; spongy grey lungs; sweetbread, because it is rare and saved for the best customers; and those goats' testicles, brought in specially from the abattoir and always presented ready wrapped, with the utmost discretion, to a certain stocky gentleman for his special treat.

About this unusual and regular order the boss and the

butcher—who treated most things as an excuse for vulgar asides—never said a word.

As it happens I knew that the two men believed that the customer acquired and maintained an extraordinary sexual power through his weekly consumption of goats' testicles. In spite of the supposed benefits of this ritual they had never ventured to try it themselves. That part of the male anatomy, so often vaunted in all kinds of jokes and comments, nevertheless demanded respect. It went without saying that one could only go so far before trampling on sacred ground.

Those goats' testicles did not fail to excite my imagination. I had never managed to see them—had never dared ask. But I thought about that chubby pink packet and about the gentleman who carried it away without a word, after paying, like everyone else, at my till (the testicles were sold for some derisory sum). What was the taste and texture of these carnal relics? How were they prepared? And above all, what effect did they have? I too tended to attribute extraordinary properties to them, which I thought about endlessly.

Translated by David Watson

Beef Steak

Martin Provost

ANDRÉ PLOMEUR WAS BORN in Quimper on a beautiful April day. His mother Fernande was larding a roast when she suddenly began to feel the way a chicken must when it's being impaled on a spit. Seeing her gasp, the client she'd been serving thought Fernande's heart had failed. But no, it was happening lower down. When her waters broke and began to run over the sawdust, they sent for Loïc at the abattoir. The father-to-be was immediately alerted that the child of his love was on the way.

Raised on whole milk, young André grew up quickly in the ancestral tradition, starting work at the butcher shop at the age of five. At seven he could handle the cash register, at eight he killed his first sheep, at ten he could bone a joint

MARTIN PROVOST (1957–) is a French writer, film director, and actor. His novels include *Bifteck* (2010), *Léger, humain, pardonnable* (2007), and *Aime-moi vite* (1992). This first chapter of *Bifteck* is set in the south Finistère region of Brittany during World War I. Note: an *araignée* (spider steak), is a prized French cut of beef roughly equivalent to a prime top round.

lickety-split and lard it butcher style while you watched. He loved meat so much, it was a joy to behold. Just as pianists are born with their talent, André seemed to have been sent to Earth with a gift for making beef steak sing.

He spent all his school years at the butcher shop, whose sign bore the family name painted in blood-red letters on a fuchsia background. When their offspring arrived, Loïc and Fernande (the direct descendent of a line of pork butchers from Molène Island who created the sausage of that name) saw no reason to change the principles of a time-tested education handed down by earlier generations. Loïc taught the boy the art of vowels and consonants. As he chopped up a carcass, he made André repeat aloud the names written on the diagrams posted on the butcher shop walls, in which neat ink drawings showed exploded views of cows, sheep, pigs, and horses. A is for appetite, B is for beef steak, C is for cutlet, D is for duck (Plomeur's also sold poultry), F is for filet mignon, G is for ground round, H is for ham, I is for indigestion, etc.

Fernande taught him to write. In this way, words like veal escalope, émincé, rib loin, shoulder of mutton, brisket, loin, chump end, haunch, and round of veal became as familiar to André as Cinderella and Snow White were to other children. He was never told a single story. What was the use of stuffing children's heads with fairy tales? asked Fernande. It just cluttered their minds and enriched the people who wrote them. When André went to bed at night, he was given a marrowbone to chew on.

The boy's very first word wasn't one of the ones you normally expect. It certainly wasn't a sweet "Papa" or "Maman," proof of the heart's desire to name one parent or the other.

André went through the normal gurgling and babbling, but the day Fernande decided to wean him, and firmly covered her breasts, the boy said something that became part of family lore forever.

"Beef steak."

"No," she corrected him logically, demonstrating his mistake on her pale skin.

To teach André to count, she exposed him to reality just as quickly. He didn't get wooden tokens or blocks to collect, or a slate on which to scrawl his first calculations. From his very earliest years Fernande instead gave him the bags of coins she carefully sorted every evening.

André quickly learned the difference between francs and centimes, displaying an innate aptitude for turning meat into money.

He never went to catechism. In his house the sight of a bloody Christ on His cross generated no more emotion than a split veal carcass fresh from the abattoir. Whether human or animal, meat meant gain; it wasn't the stuff of transcendence. Even the church bells rang only to tell the time, and for many years André thought that the faithful related to church on Sunday the same way cows and pigs did to the big market hall on Saturday.

André discovered love on the day he turned thirteen. He was precocious. Not that he was especially tormented by it, nor handsome enough that he tormented others—quite the contrary. He had blond hair, a low forehead, and round eyes trimmed by yellow lashes so pale that he looked like an albino. A soft mouth dominated a prematurely triple chin. His plump, short arms didn't appear to have elbows. Like his legs, they seemed to be pasted directly onto his trunk, without any joints.

When André was happy, he would often feel his heart with his thick, greasy fingers, and experienced an even deeper joy when he could make out his own rib steaks under the skin. But women were attracted to him just the way he was, the lucky dog. This despite his very pink skin and greasy hair—he carefully shampooed it every Sunday, but it reverted to its natural oily state by the next morning. As Fernande never tired of pointing out, having your hands in meat day and night doesn't help your cholesterol level.

The first woman to arouse André's virile inclinations was Jeannine Le Meur, a seller in the markets. One day, when André's parents were sick in bed with a nasty angina, he had just brought them a bowl of chicken soup when the shop doorbell gave its cheerful jingle.

Jeannine had a talent for snagging men. She probably also had an eye for talent, because she had barely glimpsed the young butcher when her flesh experienced a pressing need to sample his. The rhythm method was the only form of contraception used in those days, but it didn't keep people from having dangerous urges.

Spotting the barest hint of hairs more golden than the rest gleaming above André's lips, Jeannine concluded that puberty had begun its work. She promptly jumped him, and made him close the shop.

Once he had run the metal shutter down, the deflowerer had her way with him right on the old tiled floor, between scraps set aside for dogs, marrowbones, and blocks of lard.

Jeannine's lovely buttocks rolled around in the sawdust as she introduced the boy to the pleasures of the flesh—a flesh that when touched, suddenly came alive.

Until that day, André's curiosity had only led him to occasionally finger a chicken's rump or stroke a cow's teats.

When his father brought a load of offal from the abattoir to the shop (where Fernande was eagerly waiting to make her famous sausages), André never imagined that the pig testicles his sainted mother sautéed with pearl onions in a casserole could perform the same function as those hanging in his pants. What he discovered with Jeannine was the intelligent use of the heart.

Jeannine herself emerged from their encounter stunned, feeling as if she had experienced lovemaking to her very depths. Grasping that the butcher hid a true artist, she praised his talent the length and breadth of Finistère. The rumor raced through marketplaces from Quimper to Faou, Landerneau to Brest, and Plougonvelin to Roscoff that a certain young butcher had the gift of making your flesh sing.

Remember, however, that André descended from a line whose genes were passed on to him as an inheritance, like Mozart. He didn't owe his fame to his genius alone. Sometimes it takes several generations of musicians to produce a great composer.

Since 1914, the war had been sweeping up all the males in the district, so Jeannine's report quickly made André's reputation. Within a few months, a good number of Quimper women had opened their most secret parts to his famous touch. Nothing in the young butcher's looks suggested he would have so much success, but facts were facts: in his hands, female flesh definitely began to sing.

The line of housewives outside Plomeur's soon stretched to the Boénec bakery, then from the Boénec bakery to the Magadur fishmonger, from the Magadur fishmonger to the Nouveautés Parisiennes shop, and from the Nouveautés Parisiennes to the forecourt of the cathedral.

Not for a moment did Loïc and Fernande wonder about

the flood of customers. They attributed their good fortune to the fact that they had united the northern and southern parts of Finistère. After all, without Fernande, Quimper would never have known Molène sausages. But when local personalities who normally sent their housekeepers started to appear at the butcher shop—Solange Coétmieux, for example, the sub-prefect's wife, or the countess de Kergaradec in person, who stopped her carriage in front of Plomeur's, got down, and stood in line like everyone else—a kind of mystical feeling overcame the worthy Plomeur parents. Had some angel appeared to fill their coffers?

It should be noted that the war kept going, on and on. Three years had passed and the flowers in the gun barrels had long since wilted. So lonely women, the near widows and the legal ones, whether born to poverty or to wealth, all decided to come to Plomeur's and stand in line to buy their beef steak.

Each time André's fat fingers with their bitten nails began to skillfully cut a shoulder of beef, a hanger steak, or a flank steak, eager customers would press against the counter for the choicest pieces, while displaying their own.

Loïc loudly assured these hungry women that no one would leave empty-handed in spite of the war. But he knew that they all were fighting to get the *araignée,* a gourmet cut that is to beef what the oyster is to roast chicken. Because that marbled tongue of meat—firm and tender, as dark red as the secret of lips, melting, flavorful, and juicy—was the signal.

The woman who got the *araignée* knew that André would take a stroll between noon and two, when the shop was closed and Loïc and Fernande were upstairs taking a nap on their mattress stuffed with thousand-franc notes. The meeting place was always the same, behind the cathedral. The lovers recognized each other with a glance, and André would follow the chosen woman to her house, carrying the *araignée* wrapped in newspaper.

The young stud's lovemaking was apparently so energetic that being loved once by him was enough to make you feel you'd been loved forever. Did that mean that reaching the height of pleasure forever quenched the need for more pleasure? The duchesses in seventh heaven didn't soon come down from it, and many women, after this unique experience, went into retreat with the monks of Landévennec on the Crozon Peninsula, and wound up taking the veil.

His daily task accomplished, André would go home with his mind clear and his blood up. He wasn't the kind of man given to thinking about the future, but he did await the next day's quarry like a benediction. For him, life was lived in the present and only in his body, which he didn't realize might contain a soul.

Considering André's gift for making love to Breton women, one might think that he would eventually expand his field of operations to the neighboring *départements*. Alas, the ladies of Charente, Landes, and Limousin never got the chance to sample his wares.

On a beautiful November morning—as beautiful as any morning in Brittany, that is to say gray, damp, and with a sky so low you'd think it was pressing on your head like a crêpe—the local policeman announced the armistice. At the butcher shop, Loïc and Fernande rubbed their hands with glee. Returning soldiers meant greedy, starving stomachs eager for a never-ending stream of chops, pickled pork, and legs of lamb—not to mention steaks of all kinds, of course.

That morning, Fernande went downstairs first as usual, carrying her bowl of chicory coffee in one hand and a slice of bread buttered with onion fat in the other. With a swift, accurate, almost cheerful kick of her wooden *sabot*, she raised the shop's metal shutter. When she got her balance back, she stepped toward what dim light the stippled sky deigned to cast on humanity that day, planning to expose her pinched face to the drizzle and give it a bit of a wash. And then she noticed a wicker basket at her feet.

It contained a pretty baby, bright-eyed and gurgling, with a note pinned to its embroidered bib. With some difficulty, Fernande deciphered it: "This is your baby, André. He hasn't been baptized yet. Take care of him."

"What's this thing?" she asked her son, showing him the proof of his good health. An explosion of scolding, weeping, and angry threats followed. "Do you have any idea what a baby costs?" she demanded.

André paid her no mind; he had just found God. Having witnessed a second miracle—the first had occurred when the shop's customers unexpectedly opened their arms to him—he'd fallen head over heels in love with the baby. Fernande ordered him to drown it in the Odet, but received a more-than-categorical refusal. She stamped her feet in rage, threatening to grind it into sausage or pâté, but to no avail. Taking the baby under his wing, André went upstairs and locked himself in his room. He hardly came out for weeks, and then only to boil some milk.

The butcher shop's business began to go downhill. From one day to the next, André stopped all bodily commerce behind the cathedral, and the familiar long lines in front of

Plomeur's began to shrink. At first the customers, most of them widows, continued to come. Anxious about André's absence, they politely asked about him while buying their steak. But after a couple of visits, since they no longer had the object of their desires before their eyes, they began to avoid the prick of frustration by going to buy fish in the market hall instead.

Loïc and Fernande raged and pleaded with their son. They threatened to close the butcher shop forever, to sell or burn it down, even if that meant betraying their ancestors. No dice. André was on vacation. Maternity leave.

Another baby arrived, and then a third, a fourth, and so on for six months, until the last wounded veteran had come back from the war. André took in seven babies in all, and joyfully accepted responsibility for each one.

Fernande died of this, carried off by a violent attack of gout. Loïc decided to carry her coffin on his back to the pointe du Raz, hoping to return this daughter of Molène to the ocean that had borne her to him. But when the waves refused to carry the coffin away, Loïc jumped onto it like a raft, tore off his shirt, and raised it for a sail.

They say that you can still see him when the moon is full, between the pointe du Raz and the cap de la Chèvre, standing on the coffin and holding his shrouded lady butcher in his arms.

Translated by William Rodarmor

Come and Get It

Tiffany Tavernier

IT WAS TUESDAY. Marie had two days to reassert herself. She was no fool, she knew men: when a man says he wants to talk, it means it's over. Éli had made his choice. He was leaving her. But she wasn't about to let that happen, especially not over some young girl. The rush of energy Marie suddenly felt made her laugh. Just thinking of the poison in the little can stirred unsuspected strength in her.

He wouldn't make a fool of her.

Marie ran to the mirror and looked at her reflection. I'll make myself beautiful. Make myself incredibly desirable.

TIFFANY TAVERNIER (1967–) is a French novelist, screenwriter, and film director. She is the daughter of the movie director Bertrand Tavernier, for whom she and her then husband wrote the screenplays for the films *Ça commence aujourd'hui* (1999, *It All Starts Today*) and *Holy Lola* (2004). Her novels include *La Menace des miroirs* (2006), *À bras le corps* (2003), *L'Homme blanc* (2000), and *Dans la nuit aussi le ciel* (1999). The following is an excerpt from her 2008 novel *À Table!*

Blow him away! She opened her closets and pulled out the drawers, judging their contents at a glance. She would wear her little black dress, the one that was just tight enough to excite him, but not too much, because too much makes men think women want it. More than anything, men enjoy conquest. So you say yes with your body, but no with your eyes. She'll compliment him, reassure him, play the other girl's game without ever hinting at her, be incredibly sweet. Caress him. Serve the wine and the food with the gestures of a mother. Talk only about things that interest him. Agree to listen to the radio or watch television. Confuse him. Laugh; yes, laugh as often as possible, as if about a secret he'll never share. Get him to talk about his childhood. Conquer him.

Warm ratte potato salad with black Périgord truffles
Chicken with Champagne truffle stuffing
    on a bed of caramelized apples
Homemade sorbet and vanilla berlingot candies

The water was heating in a handsome copper pot. With a small paring knife, Marie finished peeling the last ratte potato with particular care, real gentleness. She was standing at the counter in a plain little slip, without any shoes. She walked lightly across the black and white tiles barefoot, wiping her hands on the cloth casually slung over her shoulder. Her combed, silky hair was pulled back, no makeup on her face, her skin very white and delicate, fresh and luminous despite the late hour.

She rinsed the newly naked potatoes and watched as the faucet's powerful stream set them dancing in the red metal strainer. On the stove, the water was boiling now.

With a skill that once came to her naturally, Marie tossed in the ratte potatoes and turned down the flame. Then she unwrapped the chicken, the sausage meat, the fine de porc, and the ground veal.

Using a small cleaver, she diced the onion, then crushed three garlic cloves with the flat of the blade. At the first rap, the glistening cloves smoothly slipped out of their skins.

Marie mixed the meats in a big bowl, tossing in some salt, several kinds of ground pepper, and some finely chopped fresh herbs. Touching the stuffing with her bare hands felt soothing. A broad smile lit up her face.

Then she opened the jar with the truffle in its juice. She cut the truffle into thin slices and slipped them under the chicken's skin. She poured the truffle juice into the stuffing, adding a little Champagne, raw mushrooms, garlic, and onion. When this was all thoroughly mixed, she stuffed it into the cavity of the chicken, which she then rubbed with butter.

The chicken was in the oven. Sitting on the now impeccably clean counter, Marie hummed to herself. A few inches away, the potatoes were chilling in ice water.

Marie pulled on a pair of heavy plastic gloves, opened a cabinet, and took out the little can marked "Poison." She set it carefully on the counter and drank a glass of wine.

The stove was hot, and the caramel was starting to firm up. Marie watched it carefully, waiting for that magic moment when it would change color, come to life. When it did, she poured it onto a sheet of marble she used for that purpose, containing the flow between two iron rulers.

The caramel was cooling and thickening fast. Marie took

a long knife, plunged it into ice water, and cut the paste into equal squares.

She was concentrating, feeling calmer than ever, even singing aloud as she grated fresh vanilla into each warm square, then twisted the berlingots into little sealed pyramids. When she came to the last square, she hesitated: should she put in all the arsenic, or just some of it? She had to decide quickly, the caramel was hardening. She hesitated one last time, and dropped in a pinch of poison, twisted up the brown berlingot and studied it, feeling half frightened, half stunned. Then she set it aside, took off her gloves, and rinsed her hands and face thoroughly. Only some of him will die, she thought. He won't know what's happening, the poison will choose what part to destroy. Marie knelt by the oven. The chicken was sizzling. She was crying. Did he have to lie to her that way? She stood up. In a childish scrawl, she wrote on the fogged window.

I'm going to kill you

Around her, the crisp chicken, the steam and smells, the poisoned berlingot in the ceramic candy dish, the rounds of sliced rattes, the apples browning in the cast iron pan, the juice of a few crushed persimmons the color of fire.

He came on time. The radio was playing, the apartment was clean, a jasmine-scented candle burned in the middle of the table. Éli came in, and before he had time to say a word, Marie took his hand and led him down the hallway without stopping in front of the bedroom door.

Surprised, he followed her.

The dining-room table was set. Smiling, she invited him to sit down.

"But . . ."

"Shhh. Not a word, Éli. You'll see, it'll be good."

He wanted to answer, wanted to screw up the courage to tell her what he had decided. She put her finger on his lips.

"I'll be right back! Meanwhile, listen to the news. I turned it to Radio-France Inter."

She snatched her little black dress out of the closet and slipped it on.

Éli had lost his composure. From down the hall, from far away, from the depths of his cowardice and weakness, he was getting impatient.

"Marie!"

"Coming, coming!"

Almost laughing, she slipped on her black stockings, grabbed her high heels and reappeared, a real woman.

He didn't know quite what to think, or why he was enjoying this game, even though it also annoyed him, or why he suddenly didn't feel well. He made to get up, but she stopped him.

"We'll have dinner first, Éli."

"Marie . . . "

Confidently, she put her finger on his lips again.

"It'll take no time at all. It's all ready."

He sat back down sheepishly. He couldn't remember ever thinking her so beautiful! She laughed, slipped a kiss into the crook of his neck, tickled him, and left again without warning.

"For heaven's sake, Marie, where are you going?"

Her hair was loose, her cleavage on display. She returned with her beautiful plate of truffled rattes and a mesclun salad, and set them down before him. Now he felt awkward.

"There's something I have to tell you."

She took his hands and stroked them.

"Don't worry, Éli. We aren't celebrating anything."

He looked at her dubiously.

"Nothing?"

"I just want to share this meal with you. All right?"

He started to smile again, looked admiringly at the dish, began to help himself.

They ate the dinner in silence. Éli was savoring the stuffed chicken, seduced by its flavors and juices. He'd had a lousy day, and this meal hit the spot.

Marie watched him chew. He was enjoying himself. Feeding him was a little like making love to him. She picked up her glass and drank some wine. Excited at the thought that she would soon be touching him, she gradually forgot about committing the crime. She threw her head back, poured herself a third glass, and suddenly decided to open a door to a fantasy she had never dared to try.

"What are you doing?" he asked.

She pushed her chair back, and slowly spread her legs.

He stood up.

"Marie, I don't have time . . . "

She opened her eyes. Éli was making a face.

"I've had too much to eat. I don't feel like it."

She stood up, feeling deeply hurt.

"Stay there. I'll get the dessert."

She could have spared him. Just a kiss would have been enough! She tossed the dirty dishes into the sink, and took the sorbets and berlingots out of the refrigerator.

She should have put in all the arsenic. That was her only regret.

Marie hurried back, set out the new dishes, and sat down across from him.

"I read the Hamas Charter on the Internet. What wackos those guys are!"

He looked at her in astonishment. Since when had Marie taken an interest in politics? He helped himself to sorbet, tasted it, and beamed at her.

"It's delicious."

Éli had just eaten his last spoonful of sorbet, and had only one thing in mind: to leave, to tell her that he wouldn't be coming next time, that he had a conference . . .

"Éli?"

He looked at her. Marie was holding the poisoned berlingot out to him. He smiled.

"You know what?" he said. "My grandmother used to make them like that!"

She was shaking, but he didn't notice. She was shaking with rage, shaking with fear. He raised the berlingot to his lips, smelled the caramel and vanilla, let it soften, didn't dare refuse Marie's outstretched fingers. How sweet she was! He had no idea why the thought was occurring to him a second time, but it was true. Her face was so peaceful tonight. She looked good enough to eat.

"Marie, I won't be able to come next Thursday."

She didn't respond. He was about to repeat the sentence but she smilingly stopped him with a gesture, as if it wasn't important.

"Do you like it?"

"Like what?"

Oh, yes, the berlingot. He laughed heartily, feeling troubled and moved.

"It's delicious, darling."

She blushed. He hadn't called her that for months. Her little-girl expression suddenly made him laugh. She followed suit. Then they couldn't stop giggling. The mood was completely relaxed. He tried to put on a serious face, wasn't able to. Neither was she. It was just like the first time.

He finally swallowed.

Ate it.

She'd pushed her chair back and was very slowly spreading her legs again. He didn't move. She had just picked up a second berlingot, licked all its facets, and held it out to him, forced it between his lips. He liked her boldness, started to suck it. She knew that she could lose him at any moment. She had to go for broke.

So she pushed her chair back and very slowly spread her legs until her tight black dress began to slide up her thighs. With a nod, she told him to check out her white panties, which were already wet.

She had forgotten about the poison. She had forgotten about the girl. He might get up at any moment.

How far is she going to go? Éli wondered. He hadn't the slightest idea, and for once she was completely beyond him.

Still smiling, Marie carefully picked up the fruit knife, the one with the small, sharp blade, and almost casually cut the top of her dress, sighing slightly. She wanted to be a nymph in Éli's eyes, a virgin, a girl of water and transparency. As it smoothly sliced through the fabric, the steel tip aroused her. Éli shivered. She was revealing his fantasy, his break with the conventional world, his black hole. He let her continue.

The fabric ripped, revealing bare skin.

To win Éli back, Marie had to get much more than his desire. She needed his essence, the most brutal part of him, something he had never given and didn't even suspect he had.

With a quick flick of the knife, Marie split her dress at chest level: the lace of her bra appeared. She moaned. She slid her hand inside the velvet cloth and stabbed it here and there. The fabric shrank, twisted, unraveled, as the cuts revealed her perfect skin, her light, her tension. Éli was perspiring. Marie handed him the knife.

"Now you do it," she ordered quietly

Éli studied the shining blade in this strange game for a long time. Then, disturbed by the heat he could feel rising in himself, he took it. Marie grabbed his hand and forced him to use it. Hesitating at first, Éli touched the knifepoint to the nape of Marie's neck, then slit the rest of the dress from her chest, leaving a slight reddish streak on her skin. She cried out softly, which excited him. God, he liked this. When he reached the elastic of her panties, he began to jab at it a little sadistically. He made Marie beg him to shred her stockings, to cut her! Her head thrown back, she implored him, offering her skin to the steel. Scratches. Lamentations.

Éli had an erection now. He couldn't take his eyes off her. It was hard for him not to split her wide open right there. He unbuttoned his jeans and started to masturbate in front of her.

Marie spread her legs still wider. Seeing Éli's hand on his stiff cock was overwhelming. She arched her back. With a quick slash, he cut first one bra strap, then the other. Her breasts tumbled out, nipples stiff.

Éli started rubbing the flat of the blade against the cottony fabric of her panties, wiping it, turning it over, pressing against her orifices, drawing a series of plaintive cries from her. She had never been so wanton: a whore in a torn dress, a bitch in shredded stockings, a sacrificial offering that only the vast heavens could recognize and glorify in this moment of fervor. He had never felt like such an animal. In rags, Marie was panting violently. He clamped his left hand over her mouth. She struggled, biting the hand that kept her from crying out. Without easing up on the pressure, he cut through the panty elastic with his other hand, suddenly freeing her lovely vulva.

Completely overcome, naked, Marie screamed. Éli dropped the knife.

"Suck me!"

She didn't obey, so he brought his cock right next to Marie's lips.

"Suck me, please! Suck me!"

In the past, she had always said yes but there, wedged between Éli knees, Marie refused to obey. He had to go further, he had to become simultaneously devouring, intimate, and devout. He had to go over the top.

Éli hesitated, now so excited that his cock hurt him. He shoved it against Marie's closed lips, wiping and rubbing across them. Marie still held out. Wild with desire, Éli yanked her hair back.

"Open your mouth!"

He was about to force her. Marie moaned, shook her head again. He lifted her chin and slapped her.

"Suck it, I said!"

With a look, Marie asked for another slap: turnabout was fair play. His cock stiff, Éli understood. He lost all control, started slapping her furiously, enjoying the domination.

"You dirty little whore! And you like it, too! Want more, don't you? Don't you?"

With her eyes, Marie begged him. To stop, to continue. To forever be the aberrant counterweight to her desire, the crazy accomplishment of the union of her soul, half of her, half of her flesh, half of her cunt and her ass. Éli was going crazy.

"Suck it, or I'm going to hurt you bad!"

She didn't do it, waited instead for the new rain of blows, the spittle on her face, his cock against her skin like a whip. She was dripping. Practically hysterical, Éli grabbed her wrists and forced her to her knees.

"I'm going to punish you, Marie."

That was when she started to yell, and the more she yelled the more he hit her. She had never felt him so bestial. He shoved her down on all fours, tore her hands free, spread her ass cheeks, and impaled her. Marie screamed. He slammed into her once, twice, then yanked his cock out, turned her over, and stared at her.

"You want some more, don't you? Say you want some more!"

Drunk, Marie nodded yes. He stuck his cock everywhere, in her vagina, her mouth, her ass, turned her over and over. Each time, she was about to come. Each time, he stopped her.

"You're my whore! Say it!"

He made her repeat it twice, three times, five times. He slapped her. She was sore everywhere. He was going out of his mind. Eyes bulging, body drenched with sweat, he buried his fingers in her ass while he penetrated her one final time, going faster and faster, trying to thrust deeper and deeper into her. She was about to come, about to cry out with pleasure.

She cried out. He clapped his hand over her mouth. She fought him, managed to get free, cried even louder. No longer strong enough to shut Marie up, Éli came as well—by her cry, in her cry, through her cry.

And collapsed.

Translated by William Rodarmor

Porcupine Stew

Calixthe Beyala

THE CHANGE CREEPS UP ON US. The weather gets warmer. Flowers spring from garden beds. Life wakes from winter as if from a bad dream. In the streets, people spill out words once frozen by the cold. They offload gestures beaten down by hail. They try to pick up the thread of their destiny once more.

Spring is here.

CALIXTHE BEYALA (1961–) was born in Cameroon and moved to France when she was seventeen. She has written many books and has won awards for *La petite fille du réverbère* (1998), *Les Honneurs perdus* (1996), and *C'est le soleil qui m'a brûlée* (1987, tr. *The Sun Hath Looked Upon Me*). "Porcupine Stew" is chapter 16 in Beyala's 2000 novel, *Comment cuisiner son mari à l'africaine* (How to Cook Your Husband the African Way). The narrator is Aïssatou, a woman in love with Monsieur Bolobolo, who lives upstairs with his aged mother in a Paris apartment building. The book doesn't tell us Aïssatou's country of origin, but Cameroon's national dish, *ndolé* (bitter leaf stew) is a recurring "dish of seduction."

People throw open their windows as if they're about to make a leap for freedom. Women beat carpets. Children chatter and grumble on their way to school. Ripening fruit glistens in the sun and its perfume floats above the apartment blocks.

There's a moment of silence, and the fire of freedom flickers inside every head.

Next thing you know, colored skirts are threading their way down the backstreets, as light as butterflies' wings. Days like these, when the sun weaves its web of good cheer around the houses, are ideal for setting the record straight.

I'm not sitting around waiting for my life to change. I cross the neutral territory of the stairwell. My neighbors are gathered at the concierge's door, sniping and bitching at each other. They're airing neighborly grudges that have lasted all winter and hanging them out to dry in their own unique way.

"Can't you turn your music down?" "Music? That's saying a lot. It's a goddamn racket! If it doesn't stop, I'm making a complaint." "And you there, what are you doing hanging your washing in the window? It's disgusting!"

I press the plastic doorbell. A mournful silence hangs in the air. It's like an abyss. Then shuffling footsteps. Then the silent abyss again.

At last the door opens a crack.

"Who is it?" asks the Mother's voice.

"I'm delivering mail from the planet Oburn. I've got something for you."

The door closes then opens again. From out of the darkness her wizened face emerges, twitching eagerly.

"Give me the mail, quickly! Hurry! It's something of the greatest importance I have to deal with straight away."

I've said the magic word: Oburn. Her fingers are trembling. I look over my shoulder, fearful.

"I can't right away. Spies have followed me here."

"Spies?"

"Yes," I say, putting a finger to my lips to silence her.

She turns away and sits down in her red armchair, looking puzzled. For the first time, I notice she's so small that her feet don't touch the floor. She takes her hen onto her lap and strokes its feathers. There are dirty bowls and jars of jam on the table. I decide to do the dishes. Over the clatter of pots and pans I hear her talking about people who are no longer with us, people she'll see again in the happy afterlife. She refers to them by name, describing their faces in such detail that she gets a lump in her throat and tears stream from her eyes, especially when she recalls a certain man called Toko.

I sit down next to her.

"So who's Toko? Come on, tell me who Toko is."

She just looks at me, without the slightest reaction. I stroke her head. Her white hair is very soft.

"I'd like to get to know Toko, see?"

She doesn't speak. The hen is as still as she is.

"Why won't you let me get a bit closer to your son? I'd like to stay here, love him, cook for him. I wouldn't take up much space, you know? And I could do things for you, too. You had your share of happiness with Toko, didn't you, but what about Bolobolo? Soon you'll be living in heaven. His life is here and it would be better if we could share it. What do you think?"

The Mother doesn't move. But her face shows the shame

and resignation of all deeply wounded people, that desire to go on living and the suffering they know will only end in death.

Abruptly, she throws the hen off. Its wings beat harshly against the linoleum. She stands up and totters toward her bedroom. The light flooding in from the setting sun makes a halo around her tiny frame. She lies down, puts her head on the pillow, and pulls the brown and white flowered bedcover over her.

"What are you doing? This illness of yours is pretty handy, isn't it? It means you get fed, housed, fussed over, with no expectation of anything in return. Am I right?"

Her expression seems more vacant than ever. But for just an instant I see a glint of astonishment.

"You're not as loony as all that, are you? Being in this state means you get to keep your son to yourself, that's all!"

She pulls the covers over her head like a scared little girl. I rip them off, forcing her to face the light. Things are what they are, and there's no point pretending otherwise.

"I love your son, and you and your illness can't do a thing about it!"

I stride back to the kitchen, singing. I feel strangely elated, as if a huge weight has been lifted off me. I recall the traditional feasts we used to have in my village. Everywhere you looked, people would be paying their respects to animals that were good to eat. We would thank them for existing in the world to satisfy human appetites. I see monkeys, birds, reptiles, deer, antelopes, each animal chosen specially for the ceremony. I see the men cutting and carving the carcasses, and the women crushing the peanuts, pistachios and chilies, while in the yard happy children scurry about amid the stench from the animals' excrement, blood, and skins. I hear the women singing softly, their breasts swinging, I see the men joining in and their songs flowing through the village like a rapturous torrent. I recall it all so vividly that my mouth starts to water for a dish of porcupine stew with wild mango nuts.

It's nighttime. The moon is setting the buildings ablaze. I set the table in obscenely lavish style, just right for kissing and wanton caresses. The divorcée from the fifth floor yells at her two monsters: "I slave away for you all goddamn day, and you don't even do your schoolwork!" Lights go on in the windows. Everything that should be home is home. Including Monsieur Bolobolo. As he hangs up his raincoat, his eyes dance at the sight of the crystal glasses and china plates on the table, which is covered with a white tablecloth lit by a red lamp.

"What are we celebrating?" he asks. Then, straight away, terrified: "Where's Maman? I don't see her."

"She's asleep."

He says nothing more. He goes to wash his hands. He talks a little about his day. He glances out the window, and we sit down to dinner. It's what I call happiness.

We eat hungrily, as if in a trance. The porcupine is delicious. We forget civilization and plunge into African savagery. We eat as we would in the tropics, with our fingers. The sauce drips from our hands. Monsieur Bolobolo makes faces at me, smacks his lips, grunts, and I understand perfectly what he means: it's good, it's hot, it's like desire. I can smell the sweet, mellow fragrance of it between my thighs, mingling with the aroma of limes and porcupine stew with wild mangoes. Now and then we giggle in anticipation of sexual pleasure. The urgent demands of our senses leave us no time to savor the banana fritters. Desire seizes our bodies with such violence that Monsieur Bolobolo pushes me against the table, sliding his hands between my thighs. I feel a sharp burning pain when his fingertips slip inside me.

"What is it?" he asks, looking worried.

Gripped by lust, I don't tell him he's forgotten to wash his hands. The sting of the chili adds strange new sensations to my desire. I shudder, and Monsieur Bolobolo makes spiral patterns deep in my belly. Any stranger finding us there, stretched out on the table between the porcupine bones and the dirty dishes, the red lamp igniting shadows across our bodies, would think we were taking part in some pagan feast.

We lie there clasping each other, panting, out of breath. I stroke behind his ears, where it's already damp with sweat.

I ask him: "So who's this Toko?"

I feel every muscle in his body stiffen. His chest swells and he stares at me, almost angry.

"Who told you about him?"

"Your mother."

He stands up suddenly and a deep crease appears at his hairline; I see it descend past his nose and come to a stop on his chin. He trudges to the armchair and lets himself fall into it. I slip quietly behind him. I start kneading and stroking the crease that is splitting his face in two. "Do you like lemon chicken?" I ask him, rubbing all the while, as if trying to get the blood back into a frozen limb.

Monsieur Bolobolo's flesh gradually relaxes beneath my fingers. It's so soft that sometimes I'm not sure it's actually there. His shoulders rise and fall, rise and fall, he shuts his eyes. A homeless man yells out some nonsense, then everything becomes strangely quiet.

"Back then," he begins, "they used to have these social events that have fallen out of fashion now: afternoon dances that brought lonely singles together to celebrate the Festival of Sacrifice, say, or just in the hope that they'd start families, get engaged, make formal marriage proposals. Maman went to one of these dances with a girlfriend. She was sad. She didn't want to dance. She sat in a dark corner. She trusted in fate because, as she said: 'The one who loves me will find me!'"

And that's where Toko found her. She said yes to him straight away because she believed in fate and God. They were inseparable for eight days, in the little apartment in the 20th arrondissement where I was born and grew up. Her faith grew stronger. On the ninth day, Toko went out to buy some cigarettes. Maman waited for him, sewing clothes for prostitutes and poor people. She kept waiting for him, there at the window, sitting at her little Singer sewing machine, because she believed life would sort itself out. She waited, but everything that happened was irrelevant or disappointing. She felt such despair that she raised her voice and howled until the ghosts back in Africa must have heard her. As she screamed, she shook her head so violently that her brain burst, scattering her memories to the four winds. From that day on, every certainty and every fact has been wiped from her mind, she has no sense of the passage of time, she can't remember life's daily routines. And that's the way Maman and the world are both headed: toward unavoidable chaos."

A cockroach crosses the room and is swallowed up by the darkness. Monsieur Bolobolo is silent now. I know I'll have to tell him some exquisite and astonishing story to draw him out of his grief.

"Have you ever eaten oven-baked *ngombo* in fresh tomato sauce?"

"Don't you ever think of anything but food?" he asks.

I stare at the wall and keep on rubbing his back.

"Food is synonymous with life. These days it's more dependable and more meaningful than justice. It might be the one source of peace and reconciliation among people."

"You're probably right," he says simply.

Love and the digestive process have worn him out. His head starts to nod. I do the only thing I can: sit between his legs and put my head on his thighs. A dazzling and almost paralyzing force takes hold of me. A strange light twinkles in my mind's eye, soft and radiant like a twilight sun. I see angels, prophets, saints and doves, and lambs being grilled over a wood fire by women in head wraps. So there I am, offering to help them, when a yell wakes me from my dream.

I turn my head and see the Mother standing there, looking at me and Monsieur Bolobolo in turn. Her face looks crooked, and I've never seen anything uglier in my life. Two tears well from her eyes and run down her cheeks. Monsieur Bolobolo rushes to his mother and puts his arms around her waist.

"What's wrong, angel?" he asks. "Tell me, sweetheart. What's upsetting you? Tell me, Maman. Please, please tell me!"

Without replying, the Mother harpoons me with her eyes. I wipe a drop of sweat from my forehead. *She wants me to leave*, I think. I stab a finger in her direction then say these words:

"Who knows what's swirling around in her head? Maybe she's rediscovered the shreds of a few happy memories?"

Monsieur Bolobolo puts his arm around her shoulders.

"Come along, my little ray of sunshine. I'm going to tell you a lovely story!" he says and leads her to her bedroom.

I clear the table and do the dishes. I sit down, feeling useless. Even the awful wallpaper with its big sunflowers doesn't distract me. I have a vague premonition of some horror I'll have to face.

"We have to stop seeing each other," says his voice right behind me.

The first thing I see is the lamplight. It's red.

I see the apartment walls papered with those big yellow flowers and feel reassured.

I see the white curtains, there at the window where they've always been.

I'm not dreaming. Monsieur Bolobolo is breaking up with me. He gives me the faintest of smiles, which only accentuates the weariness of his expression.

"Don't take it the wrong way. It's not about you."

I don't say a word. He turns me out of the apartment, and it's not just me he's chasing away, but the random nature of life. It's like an act of purification. I'm not responsible for the Mother's decline, but I'm a walking reminder of it, because I'm helping him to embrace life just as her mind is floating away into the clouds.

There are some problems in life that even the best porcupine stew with wild mango nuts can't smooth over, I would have told my mom.

PORCUPINE STEW WITH WILD MANGO NUTS

Ingredients

1 porcupine, cut into pieces
200 gr wild mango nuts
4 tomatoes
palm oil
1 onion, chopped
3 cloves garlic, chopped
1 chili
salt and pepper

Preparation

Roast the wild mango nuts. Grind them in a blender until
you have a slightly sticky paste.
Peel the tomatoes. Purée them in the blender.
In a pot, sauté the porcupine with the onion, garlic, salt
and pepper.
Add the tomatoes.
Simmer for 10 minutes, stirring with a wooden spoon.
Add five or six glasses of water.
Cover and leave to cook for an hour.
Add the mango nuts and chilli.
Stir briskly into the sauce, blending well.
Leave to cook for another 30 minutes.
Serve hot with yams.

Translated by Jen Craddock

WILLIAM RODARMOR is a veteran journalist, French literary translator, and the coeditor of the anthology *France: A Traveler's Literary Companion* (Whereabouts Press, 2008). Among his two dozen book translations, *Tamata and the Alliance,* by solo sailor Bernard Moitessier, won the Lewis Galantière Award from the American Translators Association. Recent translations include *The Book of Time* trilogy by Guillaume Prévost (Scholastic, 2007–09) and *Julien Parme* by Florian Zeller (Other Press, 2008). He lives in Berkeley, California.

TRANSLATORS

JEAN ANDERSON teaches French at the University of Victoria in Wellington, New Zealand. Since taking up literary translation in 2004, she has published over one hundred short prose works, four books translated from French to English and five cotranslated from English to French. She is the founding director of the New Zealand Centre for Literary Translation, launched with an anthology of translated prose pieces from more than twenty countries and a dozen languages into New Zealand English, entitled *Been There, Read That! Stories for the Armchair Traveller* (2008).

SARAH ARDIZZONE (née Sarah Hamp Adams) won the 2007 Scott-Moncrieff Prize for her translation of Faïza Guène's *Just Like Tomorrow* and the Marsh Prize in 2005 for Daniel Pennac's *Eye of the Wolf* and in 2009 for Timothée de Fombelle's *Toby Alone*. She specializes in translating urban slang, and has spent time in Marseille picking up North African back slang. She lives in Britain and is active in translation and school programs there.

MARA BERTELSEN has translated *The Cuttlefish*, by Maryline Desbiolles, *Tomato Sauce Love* by Sylvie Nicolas, and *Cocoa and Vanilla, the Black Gold of Madagascar*, by Ingrid Astiers. She earned her master's degree in Translation Studies from the University of Ottawa, Canada, with a focus on culinary translation, and received the Pierre Daviault Award for translation excellence. She lives and works in sunny Provence, where she is also active in local theater.

DAVID COWARD's translation of *Belle du Seigneur*, by Albert Cohen, won the Scott-Moncrieff Prize for Translation in 1996. Coward teaches at the University of Leeds and contributes to the literary pages of magazines and newspapers. He has translated the Marquis de Sade, Guy de Maupassant, Molière, Diderot, Alexandre Dumas (fils), and most recently, the novel *Waltenberg*, by Hédi Kaddour (2010).

JEN CRADDOCK translated Calixthe Beyala's novel *Comment cuisiner son mari à l'africaine* (How to Cook Your Husband the African Way) as part of her master's degree program in literary translation through the University of Victoria in Wellington, New Zealand. A journalist by trade, she has worked mainly as a radio producer and museum writer.

ROSE VEKONY translates scholarly and literary texts from French and Spanish. A certified member of the American Translators Association, she is an editor at the University of California Press.

DAVID WATSON studied languages at Cambridge University and continued his studies at Manchester. In addition to *The Butcher* and *Behind Closed Doors* by Alina Reyes and books by Agota Kristof, he also translated André Gide's famous 1902 novel *The Immoralist*. He is the author of *Paradox and Desire in Samuel Beckett's Fiction* (1991).

PERMISSIONS

The following are listed in order of appearance in this book. Every effort has been made to identify the holders of copyright of previously published material included in this book; any errors that may have been made will be corrected in subsequent printings upon notification to the publisher. The following permissions list reflects the order the stories appear in this book.

Chantal Pelletier's "Bresse" (excerpt from *Voyages en gourmandise*) © 2007 Nil Éditions. Reprinted by permission of Nil Éditions. English language © 2011 William Rodarmor.

Maryline Desbiolles's "The Cuttlefish" is excerpted from *La seiche*. ©1998 Éditions du Seuil. English language © 2001 Mara Bertelsen. Reprinted by permission of the translator.

Anthony Palou's "Fruits & Vegetables" (excerpt from *Fruits et légumes*) © 2010 Éditions Albin Michel, Paris. English translation © 2011 William Rodarmor.

François Vallejo's "Pfefferling" (from *A Table*, published by Delphine Montalant, 2004) English language © 2011 William Rodarmor.

Mariette Condroyer's "The Taste of New Wine" ("Le gout du vin nouveau" from *N'ecris plus jamais sur moi*) © 1997 Éditions Gallimard. English language © 2011 William Rodarmor.

Henri Duvernois's "The Master of Manners" ("Le maître à manger" from the collection *La Gourmandise XXe siècle*) © Henri Duvernois. English language © 2011 Rose Vekony.

Thanh-Van Tran-Nhut's "The Plate Raider" (excerpted from *Le palais du Mandarin*) ©2009 Nil Éditions. Translated and published by permission of Nil Éditions. English language © 2011 William Rodarmor.

Albert Cohen's "Belle du Seigneur" is an excerpt of *Her Lover (Belle du Seigneur)* by Albert Cohen (Éditions Gallimard 1968, Viking 1995, Penguin Books 2007, Penguin Classics 2005). © 1968 Éditions Gallimard. Introduction and translation © 1995 David Coward. Reproduced by permission of Penguin Books Ltd. and Éditions Gallimard.

Annie Saumont's "Here They Are How Nice" (excerpt from *Les viola quell Bonheur*, published by Julliard) © 1993 Annie Saumont. Translated and published by permission of the author. English language © 2011 William Rodarmor.

Laurent Graff's "Cafeteria Wine" ("Le quart de vin à la cantine" from *Il est des Nôtres*) © 2000 Éditions Le Dilettante. Translated and published by permission of Éditions Le Dilettante. English translation © 2011 William Rodarmor.

Michèle Gazier's "Paris Dinner" and "The Dining Car" (excerpts from *Abécédaire gourmand*) © 2008 Nil Éditions. Reprinted by permission of Nil Éditions. English language © 2011 William Rodarmor.

Philippe Delerm's "The Small Pleasures of Life" (originally "Petits pois," "Un Croissant dans la rue," and "Fortune du pot" all excerpted from *La première gorgée de bière et autres plaisirs minuscule*) © 1997 Éditions Gallimard. English language © 1998 Sarah Hamp Ardizzone. Reprinted by Weidenfeld & Nicolson, an imprint of The Orion Publishing Group, London.

Philippe Claudel's "Acacia Flowers" ("Fleurs d'acacia" from the anthology *A Table*, published by Éditions Stock) ©2004 Philippe Claudel. Translated and published by permission of the author. English language © 2011 William Rodarmor.